"When do you have to marry by?"

"Two months." Naomi's whispered words fell in the silent room like a hammer against a nail. If Abe had married Naomi when he was supposed to, the will wouldn't have been an issue. The *kinder* wouldn't be in danger of losing their home and each other.

He resumed his seat next to Naomi and propped his elbows on the table. "What are your terms for an acceptable marriage offer, Naomi?"

"To keep all the *kinder* here in their home, together, with me."

"No other expectations?" At her raised brow, he continued, "Do you expect your husband to remain here with you on the farm?"

"*Ach*, I never thought of anything beyond keeping the *kinder* and the farm." Color returned to her pale cheeks, and her eyes lit with a spark of curiosity. "But what man would offer marriage and not expect to live with his *fraa*?"

Abe couldn't believe what he was about to say, but there didn't seem to be any other option for Naomi and her siblings. Especially with time running out.

He took her hands in his. *"Me."*

Christina Rich lives in northeast Kansas. Her passion for stories comes from a rich past of reading and digging through odd historical tidbits, where she finds a treasure trove of inspiration. She loves photography, art, ancestry research and, of course, writing happy-ever-afters.

Books by Christina Rich

Love Inspired

A Husband for an Amish Bride

Love Inspired Historical

The Guardian's Promise
The Warrior's Vow
Captive on the High Seas
The Negotiated Marriage
The Marshal's Unexpected Bride
A Family for the Twins

Visit the Author Profile page at LoveInspired.com.

A Husband
for an Amish Bride

CHRISTINA RICH

LOVE INSPIRED
INSPIRATIONAL ROMANCE

LOVE INSPIRED®
INSPIRATIONAL ROMANCE

Recycling programs
for this product may
not exist in your area.

ISBN-13: 978-1-335-93689-9

A Husband for an Amish Bride

Love Inspired
22 Adelaide St. West, 41st Floor
Toronto, Ontario M5H 4E3, Canada
www.LoveInspired.com

Printed in Lithuania

MIX
Paper | Supporting
responsible forestry
FSC® C021394

God is love; and he that dwelleth in love
dwelleth in God, and God in him.
—*1 John* 4:16

Fleda, thank you for leaving behind a legacy
of kindness and beauty.

Dawn BonHam Bush and Henry Bush,
thank you for all your help, and answering
all my strange questions. And thank you
for your enthusiasm over this project.

Carol and Keith Land, thank you
for your support and encouragement.

Brian, my inspiration, my hero, thank you
for all you do. Your encouragement and support.
Thank you for keeping me on track with my
deadlines, for cooking and cleaning, for being my
cheerleader, for helping me believe in myself
and helping me know I AM ENOUGH.
Most of all, thank you for loving me.

Chapter One

Naomi Lambright hobbled toward the dangling clothes-line and sighed at the clothes lying on the ground. The *kinder*'s black mourning clothes, mingled with the white aprons on the wheat-colored tuffs of dormant grass, mocked the battle in her heart.

Soon, she and her younger siblings would shed the clothes, but at what cost? The farm? The *kinder*?

If she did not marry before their mourning period was over, Naomi would lose everything. It was her *daed*'s will. His last wish. She bent to gather the clothes and pressed little Daniel's shirt to her face. If she accepted any of the offers the bishop had presented so far, Daniel would be sent to a distant relative, as would Zeke. It seemed none of her prospective grooms wanted a five-year-old boy who couldn't speak except with what little sign language they tried to teach him. Even when he did use them, the jerky movements were hard to understand, even for Naomi, who attempted to work with him every day. Her potential husbands certainly didn't seem to want Zeke, a rambunctious three-year-old. She tossed their shirts into the basket and worked on gathering her sisters' dresses. The smaller ones well-worn from being handed down from sister to sister. Naomi clenched the small black fabric in her hand and brought it to her nose. This one had belonged to her, then to each of her four younger sisters, ranging from fifteen to seven, when the occasion warranted. Except for Abigail. She would have been twenty-two, a year younger than Naomi. The dress had been Naomi's first memory of wearing mourning. Almost eighteen years had passed, and Naomi still felt the hole left by Abigail's sunny presence. Of course, her sister had been close to her in age and they'd been each other's playmates, and then she was gone, all because Naomi hadn't been quick enough to pull her back into the store before an *Englischer*'s car swept over her.

How had an *Englischer*'s vehicle changed the course of their family, not once but twice? The first being Abigail all those years ago, and then her parents, almost a year ago now.

She held out the small black dress for one last look. Soon, Annie, only seven and the youngest of her sisters, would outgrow it and it would be packed away, too. Until another little girl came along, or until Naomi saw fit to give it away.

Sighing, Naomi dropped the dress into the basket. When she married, would her husband have a little girl who could wear the dress? She cringed at the thought. Only one of the marriage offers she received allowed Caleb to come with her. There were no concessions made for the others. At twelve, Caleb could work hard. Daniel and Zeke were too young for the more difficult farm work. And the girls? She didn't understand the reasoning behind her suitors' refusal to allow the girls a place in their home. Especially since Rachel, who was fifteen;

Hannah, Caleb's twin; and Sara eleven, could all keep house. But if Naomi didn't marry before the deadline, she'd be forced to send all her siblings to distant relatives. Strangers. The older *kinder* would adjust. They would understand, better than Naomi, she supposed, but the younger ones—a terrible ache sliced through her chest at the thought of sending them away—they would forget their life here, forget Naomi, too. At least she would have Caleb.

It didn't seem right, and she couldn't help wondering if Abe Dienner hadn't taken off before their wedding two years ago, she'd still have to choose between the biggest parts of her heart. Then again, if she hadn't been born with a twisted foot that often left her slow and unstable on her feet, *Daed* wouldn't have felt that she was unfit to care for the farm and all the *kinder*.

And she would be more than capable of repairing the clothesline without hesitation.

She lifted her face to the morning sun. Her breath pressed into the cooler air, and then she drew in a shaky breath. The scent of decaying leaves and freshly harvested fields was proof they were deep into fall. Soon winter would knock on their door, and they would hang the clothes inside to dry, but for now they'd take advantage of the spring-like weather.

With trembling hands, Naomi carefully climbed the ladder leaning against the T-post, making sure her foot didn't catch the side and knock her over. Once at the top, she reached out for the frayed rope and carefully threaded it through the hole of the clothesline pole and then tugged it taut until the remaining clothes on the line cleared the overgrown grass. She looped the rope as if tying off one of her quilts and pulled the rolled knot tight. Pieces of the frayed rope spun, but Naomi held on to it with what strength she could muster. The line snapped. The force flung Naomi's arms over her head. The ladder rolled away from the post, and her twisted, awkward foot caught in the rung. Her leg slipped through, the rung jabbing into her knee. She cried out and tried to reach for the post, but the ladder tilted back. Her arms flailed as her body raced toward the ground.

"Umph." Air rushed out of her lungs as her shoulders hit the ground and the ladder landed on her.

Dazed, she stared up at the brilliant blue sky, dotted with puffy white clouds, and waited for her breath to return. After a long gasp, she turned and noticed how close she'd come to the tree stump. Another two inches and she would have hit her head. *Denki, Gotte!* For sure and for certain, it was not *Gotte*'s will for her to be seriously injured, leaving the young ones without another caretaker, only ten months after the death of their parents.

Sputtering, she clenched her fists around the ladder and untangled herself from the hard wooden pieces. She fought back the angry tears pushing their way past her resolve to not cry while the sun shone. Enough tears were shed into her pillow at night, and she vowed to never allow the *kinder* to see her cry.

How could she have been so stupid? She cut the thundering fear from her chest and slowed her breathing. A twisted ankle or, worse, a broken leg would have kept them in a bind, leaving her unable to do her share of the chores, and it was already difficult keeping up with them. Who was she kidding? A terrible injury would have half the county and all their distant relatives telling her she should have married and pointing out she was too young to care for so many *kinder*. The other half would quickly divide the *kinder* among them. The farm belonged to her *brudres* and *schwesters*. It was their home, and they belonged on the farm. How could she marry any man who expected her to send the *kinder* to live with relatives? Not a single man showed interest in courting her before her parents' death except Abe, and he'd left the community without a word.

She sighed.

The farm lured in the single Amish men of Garnett, Kansas, and the surrounding communities liked Amish baked goods and those lured the *Englischers* to the roadside markets. And she felt like a sideshow spectacle.

She rolled one leg, then the other. The twisted and bent one. It sent a sharp pain through her ankle and up to her shin, straight to her knee. She pounded her fist against the hard ground as she emitted a low growl. She needed to do better. If she was going to keep the *kinder* together, she had to do better for them.

"I will lie here a moment. Two minutes. Then all will be well," she told herself. *Please,* Gotte, *let everything be all right. We can't afford an injury. Not now.*

It was disheartening to know the *gmay* was waiting for her to give up and let the *kinder* go. It would probably be easier on her if she did, but she couldn't bring herself to give up. She loved them too much. They were her heart. The *gmay* meant well. She knew that, but what they thought best for her *brudres* and *schwesters* contradicted what Naomi wanted. What she needed. She could not—would not—allow the Lambright *kinder* to be divided among mere strangers, even if they carried the same blood.

Tearing them apart could not be *Gotte*'s will, could it?

I need a helpmate, Gotte. *One who does not mind the* kinder *and will work hard.*

A shadow drifted over her. Shielding the sunlight from her face. Rose, one of their milk cows, nibbled the grass beside Naomi's arm.

"*Ach, jah,* you have a sense of humor, sending an escape artist to my rescue."

A hearty chuckle startled her, and then a strong, calloused palm reached toward her to help her up. She sucked in a sharp breath and tried to sink farther into the ground. Naomi's gaze slid past Rose's boney black-and-white shoulder to find the silhouette of a man looking down at her. She shielded her eyes for a better look, and her heart nearly stopped beating all together.

"Hello, Naomi."

She sucked in a sharp breath. For sure and for certain, she had hit her head harder than she'd thought because there Abe Dienner stood in a dark pair of pants, his chocolate-colored eyes standing out against a light green shirt, looking as handsome as ever. Suspenders fit snug over his broad, muscular shoulders. Brown curls spilled from beneath his hat, teasing his collar. His bare cheeks no longer held the chubbiness of youth, but the sharp angles of a man. A handsome man, too.

Lifting onto her elbow, Naomi ran her fingers over her head and beneath her *kapp,* searching for a bump. Because hitting her head was the only explanation for why Abe Dienner stood in front of her, holding on to Rose's halter with one hand and a rather worn-out suitcase in the other. Why was he here? She thought he'd left Garnett for good. If he was here to offer marriage as so many others had the last few months, she would pick herself up off the ground and chase him off their property.

Hysterical laughter bubbled inside her until it spilled forth. What a grand way to keep the morning on track with one disaster after another. The corner of his mouth quirked on one side. He looked at her as if she'd lost her mind, and maybe with all the worry plaguing her about which husband to choose, she had.

"What are you doing with Rose?" she asked.

Ridiculous as it was, it was all she could think of saying. Rose always found a way out of the enclosure, and they were forever chasing her down, hoping they'd catch her before someone else did. Naomi would have to see about securing the latch on the gate.

"I found her out on the road," Abe said, dropping his outstretched hand to his side when she refused his help.

That was not the answer she wanted. She wanted to know what *he*, Abe Dienner, was doing back in Garnett and why he was on her farm looking more handsome than ever. Before she could ask, the slamming of the screen door jolted her to awareness.

Zeke, her three-year-old brother, collapsed onto his knees beside her and asked, "Nomi, you die, too?"

She caught the look of concern in Abe's eyes, and she drew in a breath for courage. "No, *liebling*, I did not die, too."

He stroked his little fingers over her brow, his little puffs of breath mingled with the frosty morning air smelling like a blueberry muffin. She blinked away the discouragement weighing heavy on her chest and pasted on a smile, not for Abe's sake, but for Zeke's. She had to keep up the facade for her siblings. They couldn't see the sadness in her heart. It was the only way to keep them from being sad, too. She clasped Zeke's little hand in hers and said, "Please, help me up, Zeke."

"Here, let me."

Faster than she could reject his offer, Abe had closed the distance between them and clasped his hands under her arms until she was leaning against him for support. Black licorice, a scent she'd come to think of as only belonging to Abe, filled her, and memories of their courtship flooded her. Sitting beside him in the buggy. Holding hands as they took walks after lunch with her family. The joy she'd felt back then, with the promise of a future with the man she thought she loved, threatened to overwhelm her, until she recalled the aftermath of his rejection. The only memory of Abe Dienner worth holding on to was his broken promise. Of that she was certain.

She snagged hold of the T-post and waved him off. *"Denki."*

Abe stepped back, but kept a careful eye on Naomi, inspecting her for injury. He didn't see anything beyond her refusal to place weight on her foot and the obvious distress marring her brow and crinkling the corners of her eyes.

Blond curls sprung from her *kapp* and danced in the midmorning breeze. Her apron held the hint of egg and flour from the morning baking. And even though the black dress told him she continued to mourn her parents, she was like sunshine on his face after months of dark clouds and heavy rain. The sight of her bare feet this late in November nearly made him smile. And for one small moment, it felt good to be home, but Garnett wasn't his home anymore. He didn't belong here. His *daed* made that clear.

"I am sorry about your parents."

Naomi's bright blue eyes widened. They held him, and he was unsure if he'd said the wrong thing, but he couldn't think of anything else to say to break the awkwardness between them. Mentioning her parents' deaths had obviously been inappropriate. He shuffled the toe of his boot into the shin-high grass. The accident had been over ten months ago.

"I'm sorry, I shouldn't have said that." His apology was long overdue and nothing more than a reminder she probably wanted to forget. The stack of letters he'd begun to write to her remained on the small desk next to the oil lamp in the room he used at his cousin's home. His intentions had been good and real, but each time after penning her name, he lost the courage to write more.

He would have returned for the funeral, but he was uncertain if his presence would cause consequences for *Mamm* and Levi. Besides, even though he'd been taught to turn the other cheek, he hadn't been ready to face his *fater* or the anger that continued to stir whenever he thought of seeing *Daed* again. Even now, the urge to ball his fists was strong. Only the gnawing in his gut these past weeks, and Aunt Esther's concern at not having seen *Mamm* in a while, had propelled him to come back to Garnett. He needed to see with his own eyes that Levi and *Mamm* had suffered little during his absence.

He cleared his throat and was about to say more when the black-and-white milk cow he'd found roaming the road nudged him. Reaching out, he rubbed the cow's nose and asked, "She goes in the field beside the big white barn, *jah*?"

The Lambright farm hosted two large barns and a few smaller outbuildings. The large white barn had been used to milk the cows and house the two draft horses used for plowing the smaller fields. The bigger metal building was used for various other things such as woodworking and mending broken implements. Naomi's father wasn't against some modern conveniences. He even had a tractor for the larger fields, but he'd once told Abe he believed in teaching his sons the old ways, too. Knowledge is good, *jah*? And knowing there is more than one way to get the job done, and having the ability to do them, is wise, Jeremiah Lambright had said.

Naomi bobbed her chin and held her hand out to the small boy squatting in the grass, inspecting something crawling on the ground. "Come along, Zeke. We should go to the house."

Zeke jumped up and took her hand. Naomi cried out the moment she put weight on her leg and fell against the clothesline post. Her knuckles burned white around the pole. Etched pain sharpened the soft contours of her oval-shaped face.

Abe reached toward her and laid his hand on her shoulder. "You're injured."

She flinched away from him and bit out, "I. Am. Fine."

"Nomi hurt." Zeke gazed up at him in concern.

"Yes," Abe said.

"No," she replied with less bark and more calmness. "I am fine."

"You can't stand on your leg."

She scowled at him. Tears filled her eyes. Were they hurt tears? Frustrated? Or were they angry ones directed at him? Did she wish he would leave?

"Come," he said as he wrapped her arm over his shoulder and supported her weight. "I'll help you to the house."

He was pleased when she didn't argue, but also concerned. The woman he remembered had always been strong-willed and determined to do things on her own, never asking or expecting help. He'd admired that in her. That had drawn him to her, and spurred him to ask her for buggy rides and sit next to her during singings.

He should have known better, though. He should have known, deep in his heart, he couldn't marry without subjecting a woman to the life his mother had lived. He feared becoming his *daed* and the night he'd left Garnett, he knew his biggest fear had come true when he'd nearly hit his *fater* to get him off his *bruder*, Levi. As it was, Abe had thrown his *daed* off, slamming him into the wall. He shuddered with shame at his behavior. He should have found a way to intervene without violence.

He pushed the memory away and helped Naomi sit on the white wooden chair nearby, and then, crouching, he cupped the area beneath her calf, her skin cool from being outside. He looked into her eyes and asked, "May I?"

At the flush of her cheeks, he thought to leave her alone, but she nodded. He gingerly ran his hand over the baseball-sized ankle. He emitted a whistle and glanced up at her. "You need a doctor."

She shook her head. "I can't."

"If it's the money—"

"No!" she said, her fingers twisting in her apron. "I can't go to the doctor."

"Naomi," he said, not understanding her refusal. "This looks bad."

"I know," she responded with more tears. "I've endured the ugliness of my foot my whole life."

He shifted on the balls of his feet, uncertain how to reassure her he didn't find anything about her ugly. She was beautiful. He'd always thought so, but it had been more than her delicate beauty that had drawn him to her; she had an inner strength and courage. And even more so, she never used her slightly uneven gait as an excuse for idleness. She always worked harder than others whenever they gathered for community events, never sitting or taking breaks. She always bustled around like a tiny hummingbird. Tendrils of sorrow brushed against his conscience. If only he hadn't been born Abe Dienner, then maybe he could have married her. But married life wasn't for him, his *daed* made certain of that.

Abe drew his hand over the swelling of her ankle and beneath the curve of her foot. He knew from one of their nightly walks she'd been born with a club foot that stubbornly refused to respond to any of the remedies her parents had tried, and although Naomi's father didn't mind certain modern conveniences, he didn't trust the *Englischer* doctors. Was that why she didn't want to go? His fingers tensed over the purpling flesh. "No, Naomi, your ankle is swollen. You need a doctor."

"Please, I can't." Watery blue eyes tore into him, scratching at walls he'd erected when he'd left Garnett. "No one can see me like this."

"But, Naomi…" he said.

"No." Her small whisper tugged at him, working him like a plow to the ground. He didn't understand her reasoning, but decided he wouldn't press the issue.

Zeke's tiny hand fluttered against Abe's thigh. Abe glanced down at Naomi's little *bruder* crouching next to him, his dark eyebrows pressed together in worry. "Nomi okay?"

Abe's breath hitched at the *kinder*'s question, but he didn't need to answer him as the boy soon became distracted by an insect, and crawling on his hands and knees, Zeke followed the bug across the porch. For a moment, Abe wished life was as simple as examining bugs through a child's eyes, but he wouldn't want to repeat his childhood and the pain inflicted upon him all those years.

Dislodging the memories from his thoughts, he took a cushion from the rocker beside Naomi and propped her foot on a milk crate. Her pleading eyes warred with what he knew should be done, but he felt he owed her for leaving her as he had, with no explanation. But he couldn't have shared the burden of his shame or the dark secrets of the Dienner family, not with anyone, not his aunt, not the bishop and especially not with Naomi. She would only have touched the back of his hand in that gentle way of hers and stubbornly offered understanding and kindness until he accepted it. Naomi Lambright was, by far, too good for the likes of him.

He stood and hooked his thumbs around his suspenders. She needed a doctor, but he couldn't refuse the pleading in her eyes. "All right, we won't go to the doctor, for now," he said as he glanced around the farm for a buggy or anything he could use to get her to town if she changed her mind. He thanked *Gotte* when he noticed the old blue tractor Naomi's father had used for farming, parked next to the buggy with a bent wheel. *Gut*, they weren't without transportation, he thought. "However, I can't promise I won't load you up on the tractor and take you to town if I feel it's necessary."

Her jaw fell open and her shoulders pulled straight as a yardstick. "You wouldn't!"

"*Jah*, you have my word on that," he said, keeping his tone flat, so she understood he was serious.

Abe flinched at Naomi's snort. He studied her as the angles of her shoulders sharpened and she snapped her head high. "I suppose I have nothing to worry about then."

He tilted his head to one side and scowled. "What do you mean by that?"

A younger, much shorter version of Naomi burst through the screen door on a scented wave of fresh, buttery baked bread. Abe's stomach grumbled, reminding him it had been hours since he'd eaten. The girl crossed her arms and cocked her hip. "Have you finally come to marry my sister, then?"

Chapter Two

"Sara!" Naomi clasped her sister's wrist and gently tugged her closer. "Apologize."

"But he broke his word to you."

Naomi's eyes widened, and she darted her gaze toward Abe. Her cheeks held an adorable rosy hue, but Abe didn't know if it was from her injury, anger, embarrassment or the chilly breeze.

Finally, Naomi drew in a breath, then wrapped her arm around her sister's waist. "That is a matter between me and Abe."

He felt thankful Naomi wouldn't reprimand him, too, and his shoulders sagged beneath the suspenders holding up his broadfall pants. "Sara, your *schwester* needs ice for her ankle. Is that something you can do while I secure the cow?"

Sara nodded, and Naomi slumped against the back of the chair until her spine met the wooden curves. She blinked at Abe. *"Denki."*

He shrugged. "What for?"

"Giving her something to do. The girl has more questions than I know how to answer."

As if he knew what she meant, he said, "Sara is right.

I broke my word, and I owe you an explanation, but it isn't something I can give. I'm sorry, Naomi, but that is all I can say. My reason for leaving isn't my own to tell."

"I understand."

"How can you? It isn't something even I understand." He turned away from her and gazed up at the blue sky. It had taken months for him to come to terms with *Gotte*'s will in his life and the cruelty he, his *bruder* and *Mamm* had suffered under the fists of a man claiming to fear *Gotte*. He still didn't understand, nor did he understand his *mamm's* willingness to remain in her circumstances, but he'd come to peace with *Gotte*, and that was all that mattered, he supposed. "I'm in need of a place to stay tonight. After I visit *Mamm*, would you mind if I bed down in the barn?"

The tendrils springing from her *kapp* began to shake, and he feared she would say no, but he quickly interrupted. "I noticed a fence in need of repair, and the lawn needs cutting. I wouldn't ask to stay for free."

Wide blue eyes stared back at him.

"Think about it, *jah*?" He adjusted his hat and stepped off the porch. "I'll go take care of the cow."

"Rose," Naomi said. "Her name is Rose."

"*Jah*, I remember," he said, then strode toward the cow. He stopped and turned toward her. "It was good seeing you again, Naomi. If you choose to not let me stay, I hope one day you'll forgive me."

She pulled away from the back of the chair. "You're not staying in Garnett?"

He shook his head. "*Nae*, I'm only here for the night."

He felt her gaze on his back as he took Rose's halter in his hand. There was so much to say between them, yet so much he couldn't say. He stepped into the cold shadow of the barn and wished he'd put on his coat instead of folding it into his suitcase. He lifted his hat off his head and speared his fingers through his hair. Sun shone through parts of the roof where it shouldn't, and gates hung at odd angles. He then took a walk down the main aisle of the barn. His teeth gnashed together. Milk buckets lay on their sides on the floor, instead of hanging on their nails, posing a hazard to anyone who needed to walk around them. Every stall door hung loose on its hinges. He'd seen the broken fence and clothesline, the yard, but this was much more than a night's worth of work. He thought about the other barn. Was it in bad shape, too? What of the smaller outbuildings used to store feed and other necessities?

As if those repairs weren't enough, he'd seen many others as he'd walked around. Some of the fencing had slid from the nails that kept it in place. Another area looked as if the wire had been cut, and he couldn't help wondering how Naomi had let the farm fall into such disrepair. No wonder the milk cow had escaped. Thank *Gotte* only one had. The rest seemed content nosing the hay bale haphazardly cut instead of loose and free in the trough for easy access.

Tracing his steps, he tried not to see all that needed to be done, but every little thing out of place called out to him, forcing his hands to clench into fists. There was no way Naomi's *daed* had left things like this. He'd been meticulous, and he would have taught Caleb the proper way of things. Abe rolled his shoulders, forcing the muscles to relax. The boy was only eleven or twelve at the most, old enough to know the right way of things, yet young enough to let chores slide to have more time for play.

Did Naomi know what shape the barn was in? She probably wouldn't recognize the multitude of problems here, and he didn't have enough daylight to do all that needed to be done, especially if he intended on seeing *Mamm* and Levi tonight. But how could he justify leaving Garnett until the barn was set to rights and he made certain Caleb understood the importance of keeping up the chores and putting things back in their proper place. Would Naomi allow him to stay? That didn't matter. He wasn't leaving until things were back as they should be. He owed her that much.

Abe grunted. This hadn't been his plan, but it was as good as any, and maybe what little help he offered would soothe the inconvenience Naomi experienced over his leaving two years before. Although, he wasn't sure anything would soothe the pain she might have felt from his actions. The way she refused his help and glared at him, she was still upset. *As she should be, you fool.* He snagged a bucket of tools from the floor and made his way to the broken gate Rose had pushed through to her freedom, and then he set about fixing each of the fasteners on the individual stalls inside the barn until he was lost in thought. This was natural to him, and far preferable to stocking shelves and sweeping floors at his cousin's store. He was grateful for the work and the place to stay in Haven, but he'd missed farming. More than he had realized.

"Abe!"

He swiveled on the balls of his feet, the pair of pliers he'd found buried in a bucket gripped tight in his hand. Deep in thought, he'd forgotten whose barn he was in and whose gate he repaired. The panic-stricken girl startled him, near out of his skin. Had she come to badger him about marrying Naomi again? He finished twisting the wire and stood. His eye caught yet another loose hinge on another door.

"What's the matter, Sara?"

"My *schwester*."

Thinking Naomi had hurt herself again, Abe pressed his lips into a firm line. Stepping out of the shadows of the barn, he headed toward the house, but someone tugged on his arm. He glanced down at a little girl he assumed was Annie, who had to be seven or eight by now, then caught the rest of the Lambright *kinder* staring at him. They'd all grown , and somehow that surprised him, as if he'd expected them to remain the same for the past two years.

"She won't be in the mood to see you," Sara said, standing beside Annie with her arms crossed. "It's all your fault, you know."

He blinked. "My fault? I didn't cause her to fall."

"*Ach, jah.*" Caleb popped out from behind a barren tree and rocked back on his heels, bare toes pointing upward as he did so. The boy had grown a foot since he'd last seen him and would no doubt be tall like his *daed* had been. "She's been in a mood for a while."

"What sort of mood?" Abe asked.

"Depends on when you catch her," Hannah said, slipping from behind the tree her twin *bruder* had just vacated. "She might be mad."

"Might be crying," Annie added.

"Crying?" It didn't surprise him Naomi still grieved

over her parents, but how was he to fix that? He looked over his shoulder toward the porch to see if Naomi still sat in the chair. She wasn't there. His jaw tightened. Why wasn't she sitting with her foot propped? Had she gone off somewhere to cry? The thought of her crying unsettled him.

"For sure and for certain, she worries the bishop will show up with another marriage proposal, and after falling off the ladder, well, she just might give him an answer." Hannah grabbed Caleb's wrist and dragged him back into the barn.

"Another?" he asked, digging in his heels.

Annie held up her hands and ticked off her fingers until she counted to six.

"Six marriage offers? Why so many?"

Sara's lips puckered. Crossing her arms, she approached him. "Naomi won't be happy we told you, but she has to marry before our mourning time is over or we'll lose the farm."

"And us," Hannah said.

"We'll get sent to some aunt or cousin," Caleb added.

"I don't want to go." Annie's bottom lip quivered.

Abe's jaw fell open. "Who said she has to marry so soon? Why?"

"It's in *Daed*'s will. If she doesn't marry, she has to sell the farm and then choose which relative each of us will be sent to," Hannah said.

Abe didn't know what to say. It all seemed cruel, and no wonder Naomi had been adamant about not being injured and trying to do things herself. No wonder she was mad at him. No wonder the *kinder* blamed him.

"I assume she's refused them all."

"Jah." Rachel, the next oldest after Naomi, appeared out of nowhere and said, "And rightly so."

One thing Abe knew about Naomi, family meant everything to her. It was one of the things that originally drew him to her. "Why doesn't she choose one and keep you all together?"

Rachel's cheeks darkened a shade, and her left eyebrow flew upward, reminding him of her older sister when she was piqued. "Not all things are as simple as that, Abe Dienner. If you'd stayed around and married her as you'd promised, we wouldn't be in the predicament we are now. Naomi wouldn't have to decide which of us will be thrown out with the bath water."

The fifteen-year-old fisted her hands and marched away. He turned his attention to Hannah, who shrugged. Sara mimicked her older sister's actions and fisted her hands on her hips, too, but instead of marching off in anger, she glared at him. Caleb hooked his thumbs into his suspenders and dug his bare toes into the dirt. It was obvious they weren't going to tell him any more. Abe glanced at the house and wondered which mood Naomi was in. He could face her anger. But he couldn't deal with her tears. As a friend, he would offer her assistance and maybe help her decide which marriage offer she should accept.

Heading to the house, a gaggle of her siblings following close behind, he found her sitting at the kitchen table, staring intently at a piece of paper. "Naomi."

Startled, she looked up at him.

"Would you like to talk?" He pulled out a chair and sat next to her.

She looked past his shoulder to the *kinder* and tilted

her head. "It's not mealtime, yet. You all have chores to do. Rachel, you should be on your way to work, ain't so? And don't forget to take the finished quilts to the consignment shop. It is a busy time, these weeks before Christmas, and the *Englischers* like our work."

"*Jah*, Naomi, of course."

"Naomi, please don't ignore me," Abe said, reaching to take the list from her shaking hands. "Something has upset the *kinder*."

"The quilts—"

"Will wait."

She hung her head.

"I understand you must marry soon or lose the farm and the *kinder*."

Naomi snapped her gaze to his and then to her siblings standing behind him. He perused the names on the list. Some of them were suitable options, but he couldn't imagine her married to any of them. Especially Jacob Haver. And why were some of the *kinder*'s names not listed beside them? "Naomi, what does this mean? Why is Caleb's name listed beside all the marriage offers and none of the others?"

Lifting her head, she stared at him blankly. "That is the *kinder* they will accept with our union"

He looked the list over again, disbelieving any man would ask her to give up any part of her family. However, he understood the necessity. Jacob was too old to care for Zeke and Daniel. And last he knew, John Yoder had over twelve *kinder* of his own. Caleb would be old enough to work hard.

He laid the list on the table and stood. He paced toward the sink and crossed his arms. He glanced at each of the *kinder*. Rachel, Hannah, Caleb, Sara, Annie, and then to Daniel and Zeke, who sat on the floor near Naomi's feet, playing with their wooden animals. He drew in a long breath and released it as slowly. "Obviously, you can't marry any of them."

Silence met his ears.

"When do you have to marry by?" he asked.

"Two months. After the New Year." Her whispered words fell in the silent room like a hammer against a nail. His heart thudded in his chest and crept into his throat. No wonder Sara and Rachel seemed angry with him. If he had married Naomi when he was supposed to, the will wouldn't have been an issue. The *kinder* wouldn't be in danger of losing their home and each other.

He resumed his seat next to Naomi and propped his elbows on the table. "What are your terms for an acceptable marriage offer, Naomi?"

Her lips pressed into a firm line, but then she drew in a soft breath, one that seemed to release the tension from her shoulders. "No one has asked me that."

"Well, I am. What are your terms?"

"To keep all the *kinder* here in their home, together, with me."

"No other expectations?" At her raised brow, he continued, "Do you expect your husband to remain here with you on the farm?"

"*Ach*, I never thought of anything beyond keeping the *kinder* and the farm." Color returned to her pale cheeks and lit with a spark of curiosity. "But what man would offer marriage and not expect to live with his *fraa*?"

Abe couldn't believe what he was about to say, but there didn't seem to be any other option for Naomi and her siblings. Especially with time running out. She needed a man to stand beside her. Nothing more, which was the least he could do.

He took her hands in his. "Me."

Naomi's pulse beat against her chest, filling her throat. Did she fear his pity? No, she feared she couldn't trust him. That he was still as fickle as he had always been, and that he'd change his mind and leave before their wedding, just as he'd done before. Then she'd be in the same predicament. In need of a husband before the mourning period was complete. She shook her head. She couldn't agree to marry him, could she?

"Before you say *nae*, please hear me out." Motioning toward the screen door, he lifted his hat from his head. Chestnut curls sprung out in all directions, and she recalled how much she liked his unruly curls and the way the wind teased the locks spilling from the brim of his hat as they went for rides in the open buggy. He clamped his hat back on his head and said, "The barn is in shambles, ain't so?"

When she didn't respond, he looked at her. She nodded. Both barns were, and she didn't even know where to begin.

"You need help, and I can do that."

She dropped her foot from the chair next to her and winced at the jagged pain searing her ankle and rippling up her leg. The towel filled with ice plunked on the hardwood floor with a resounding thud. It mocked the vice-like fear squeezing her chest. Would Abe keep his word or would he walk away again?

His previous abandonment two years ago floated in

her thoughts. She couldn't trust him, could she? She leaned against the table and tried to stand, but a sharp pain sliced up her leg. She fell back into the chair. "I don't need your help, Abe. Besides, I have nothing to offer you in exchange."

She feared that was the most likely reason he'd left the first time and was too kind to hurt her feelings, but she wouldn't voice her thoughts to him.

"You're wrong, Naomi." Pulling his hat from his head again, he dropped his gaze to the list and curled the brim in his hands. "You have plenty to offer any man, which is why I suspect you have so many offers."

She gulped, wondering what had him nervous. Was his offer out of pity and nothing more? Did it even matter? As appealing as his offer was, she couldn't trust him. "They've come at the prospect of what *Daed*'s farm is worth."

"I doubt that, Naomi. You would make a *wunderbar fraa*. However, none of these men…" he said, poking his finger at the paper. "None of them meet your requirements for a marriage. But I do. You can abide by your *daed*'s will, keep the farm and the *kinder*. While I'm in Garnett, I need a place to stay. There is plenty of space in one of the barns. A room and meals in exchange for setting the farm to rights and my last name."

The compliment heated her cheeks, but it was the reiteration of his offer, giving them everything they needed to stay in their home, and without seeking to use the farm for his own inclinations, that began to thaw her heart.

Hope cast distrust to the side like a wormy tomato to the compost. She chewed the tip of her nail. How could she allow this opportunity to pass? Another one this good hadn't come in the months since the deaths of her parents, and she knew another one wouldn't, not with the terms she wanted.

"You still intend on staying one night?" She stopped talking at the shake of his head.

"No, upon inspection, there is much to be done. I will stay as long as it takes to get the farm in working order and remind the boys of their responsibilities to the farm and their family."

"I don't know," she said, shaking her head. Abe staying in the barn more than one night meant he'd be underfoot and close. It meant she'd watch him from the kitchen window and woolgather over what could have been if he hadn't left Garnett, and she'd wonder at the truth as to why he offered her a marriage in name only, now, instead of a real one.

"It won't be long, just until I've made some of the more pressing repairs you need, and until I've seen my *mamm*."

"Say *jah*."

Naomi tore her gaze from his and saw four of her siblings watching her. Rachel stepped forward and dropped a hand to Abe's shoulder, all the while looking at Naomi. "Whatever Naomi decides, we'll stand by her," she said. "But we're desperate for the help, *schwester*. Abe is offering it."

Naomi wiped her damp palms on her apron and willed her pulse to settle. They did need help. Desperately, as Rachel said. And Abe's marriage proposal would see that the *kinder* would remain in their home. Naomi's heart screamed at the unfairness of it all. Gotte, *I need wisdom and help.* She twisted her fingers into her apron. Abe's offer would allow her the peace of mind she needed where the *kinder* were concerned. Before she knew what she was doing, Naomi found herself nodding.

"*Jah*, we will accept your offer." Naomi held up her hand as brilliant smiles spread across each one of her siblings' faces. She found Abe staring at her, one of his dark brows raised in question. "On the condition, you only step foot in the house for meals."

Abe rose from the chair, returned his hat to his head and stuck out his hand to shake hers. "I accept your terms."

"Woo-hoo!" Hannah jumped up and down.

"Now, I can go to work," Rachel said, bubbling over with laughter. "If Caleb will drive me in the buggy. I'm sure Abe will want the use of the tractor, and Caleb will need to pick up the supplies we need for a celebration."

"Celebration?" Naomi asked as the familiar knot tightened in her throat. Ever since the buggy accident that took their parents, she became nervous when any of her siblings took the buggy, but there was nothing to be done about it. Rachel often went to work, and Caleb had been driving the buggy for some time now. It wasn't their fault or their negligence that killed their parents, but a simple accident of an *Englischer* youth trying to avoid a dog in the road.

"*Jah!* We're having a wedding!" Sara shouted as she and Annie danced in wide circles and then clasped their arms around Abe. "Thank you, Abe, now we can stay together as a family."

"I suppose that is cause for a celebration," Naomi responded. "All right, now get going, you two, or Rachel will be late for work. And be careful."

She sensed Abe's attention on her and when she looked up, he was watching her with a solemn, apologetic look. She turned from him, not wanting his pity. He could never understand what it was like to lose his parents and fear losing another loved one.

"Thank you, Naomi," he said, drawing her attention back to him. "You don't know how much I appreciate the help, and," he said, rubbing his stomach, "I look forward to your cooking. It's been a long while since I've had a good home cooked meal."

His wink jolted her. Abe's teasing was unacceptable if she was going to survive their marriage of convenience. "I am the one who is grateful. I don't feel this is a fair exchange, but I appreciate your sacrifice for my family." She eased to her feet and shooed them out of the house. "Now, if you'll excuse me, I have chores to tend to, as do all of you."

Abe swept Daniel onto his back, took Zeke's hand, motioned for the rest of her excited siblings to follow him outside and then turned toward her. "You shouldn't be on your foot. It should be elevated and iced."

When she didn't respond, he left her to the quiet of the house, and she was thankful for the moment alone, to thank *Gotte* for His will, but to also voice her complaints. Why had Abe teased her, momentarily renewing the sense of wonder and the field of butterflies in her stomach she'd had whenever they'd spent time together? Of course, the wonder was cut short by the stinging rejection he'd left her with when he'd left Garnett. Doubts crept in her thoughts as silence settled over the house.

Should she chase after him and tell him she changed her mind? No, she'd only become flustered in his presence. He had that effect, even more so when he complimented her or held the door open for her.

She fanned her cheeks to cool them.

There had been a time when her cheeks had hurt from smiling all the time, back when Abe courted her. They'd once enjoyed each other's company, and she'd been hopeful they'd have a *gut* marriage. She leaned her elbows on the table and stared at the list. She'd never expected love from her husband, only faithfulness and loyalty and for him to be a good Amish husband as *Daed* was to *Mamm*. She would have married any of the men proposing, if they would have allowed her to keep the *kinder*. Any of them but Abe.

Now it seemed he was her only hope of keeping her siblings together, and she sure hoped she wasn't making a mistake accepting his offer. She didn't mind too much that he was eventually leaving and would allow her and her siblings to remain at the farm. All she had to do was keep her distance from him until he left. If he kept his word and didn't leave before their wedding again. There was more at stake than her pride. The *kinder*'s future was more fragile than her own emotions and feelings, and she had to set them aside for their sake. But that didn't stop her from gingerly making her way up the stairs and to her room.

She sank onto her bed for a moment to wait out the throbbing in her leg and glanced around her sparse room until she noticed the lavender-colored dress hanging on a hook. It was the dress she and *Mamm* had made together. The one she would have worn when she said her vows to Abe. He'd even taken her to town and helped pick out the fabric. She'd almost chosen a plain white, but Abe had said he liked the way it brought out the color of her eyes. She'd wanted to be pretty to him. So, she chose the purple with giddy excitement.

In the weeks leading up to their marriage, she imagined what it would be like to have their own home and to cook for him when he came in from the chores. Mulberry pie had been his favorite, and she'd hoped to plant lots of trees. She'd been nervous over the thought of all the changes.

She sighed, knowing nothing would change, and she was glad for it. This would still be her room. Reaching out, she felt the tight stitching of the hem *Mamm* had made along the cuff of her sleeve, and she stifled the memories. She swiped a tear from her cheek and allowed the dress to fall from her hand. Back against the wall as it had been all these last two years, waiting for an occasion to be worn. Useless and without purpose. Much like she'd felt since Abe had abandoned her. When he began courting her, she had held a sense of hope that she could maybe be a good *fraa*. He encouraged her and made her feel capable. He never instilled doubt in her.

Until he'd left. And then doubt followed her like a hungry puppy.

Abe had allowed her to do things on her own, and with great patience he showed her how to tie a knot and harness the horses. He'd always been there beside her, championing her in even the smallest tasks. Things *Daed* felt were too dangerous for her to know about. She'd believed Abe would honor her as a *fraa*. Those hopes had been lost the moment she discovered Abe had left town.

Now that he was back, dare she hope again?

Her bedroom door squeaked open, and Naomi turned to find Hannah and sweet little Daniel in the doorway. "The bishop is here to see you."

Naomi sighed. How would she tell him of Abe? She prayed he would grant his blessing. "I'll be down in a moment."

Hannah nodded and slipped into the hall with Daniel's hand clasped in hers. Naomi ran her hands over her dress and then dabbed her eyes with the cool cloth. She wondered if Abe would come to the house when he realized the bishop was here. She wasn't certain why, but she sensed she'd have more peace with him at her side rather than facing the bishop alone. Odd, since he'd only been in town a few hours.

Holding on to the wall, Naomi hopped down the stairs on one foot, carefully navigated the stairs, the kitchen, and then stepped out onto the porch. The bright midmorning sun caused the throb in her head to worsen. She glanced around the yard for Abe, but he was nowhere to be found. No one was. Where had they all gone?

"*Gut* afternoon," she said, catching the bishop's eye, and then eased to sit on the spindle-backed chair on the porch. She tried to sit as natural as possible to keep the bishop from suspecting her injury. She hoped the bishop's visit was short.

"*Gut* afternoon, Naomi. What are you baking today? As always, it smells delicious," he said.

She knew his compliments were meant to put her in a *gut* mood, but this morning, she felt his words were nothing more than air. "*Denki*, Bishop Mueller. Only muffins and bread."

"Wunderbar," he said, shifting his weight. "I have news."

He rushed on, and she listened intently to him as he explained the reasons she should accept yet another offer. This one from Jacob Haver's *bruder* in Missouri. None of the reasons included the *kinder* remaining in their home, or even in Garnett, but none of that mattered now.

"Jacob's *bruder* is well-established in his community."

"It is a kind offer, Bishop Mueller," Naomi said as she focused on the barn, praying Abe would appear. "But I have—"

Bishop Mueller held up his hand to stop her from voicing her rejection. "Before you say *nae*, he has stated you may keep the older *kinder*. They'll be *gut* help around his farm as all his sons have married and moved to their own homes."

"Still," she said feeling her cheeks heat. "I would be forced to send the younger ones away, and none of them, according to what you say, will remain in their home." Naomi tried to keep her tone respectful and not grind her teeth together. "I am sure he means well. They all mean well. However, all the *kinder* will remain together. Here at their home. Those are my terms."

"That is not possible. You're not being reasonable or realistic about your circumstances. And you're running out of time." He dug his fingers into his beard. "Naomi, I hope *hochmut* is not guiding you."

Pride? She clenched her hands but forced calm into her thoughts. "If *lieb* is *hochmut*, then *jah*, I suppose it is guiding me."

"I understand Abe Dienner is here. I ran into Caleb

when he dropped your sister off at the diner. He says Abe's helping fix things around the farm. You don't expect him to marry you, do you?"

Her stomach clenched. Would the bishop withhold his blessing if he knew the details of Abe's proposal? Did she need to tell the bishop Abe was set against a real marriage and that he would go back to Haven?

"I was not speaking of *lieb* in marriage, Bishop Mueller," she said, "but rather my love for my *schwesters* and *brudres*."

"I did not mean to upset you, Naomi." He adjusted his straw hat. "You have declined all the marriage offers brought to you, and the time to abide by the terms of your *fater*'s will is nearing its end."

"I am aware of the time, Bishop Mueller." She read over her copy of the will every night before her prayers, hoping to find the words had changed, but they hadn't. "*Mamm* always said difficulties were the beginnings of newfound hope. I need to do what is good for the *kinder*." Even if it meant playing the fool for Abe Dienner. Knowing her emotions were tender and raw, vulnerable even, was the very reason she'd banned him from the house, except for meals. Any time spent in Abe's presence would have her dreaming of what could have been and longing for what never was. The sooner he left Garnett, the better off all of them would be. "I did receive a marriage offer from Abe, and you will be pleased to know I have accepted it."

This time, the bishop's eyes grew wide. He opened and closed his mouth, and Naomi felt a bit of pleasure at shocking the older gentleman, when that seemed a nearly impossible task. "Please, give Jacob and his *bruder* my thanks, but *nae* all the same."

He finally settled one of his brows into a high arch. "Your parents would want the *kinder* well cared for," Bishop Mueller said. He must have noticed the flush she felt creeping into her cheeks as he rushed on to say, "That is not to say you are incapable, Naomi, but Abe has proven to be fickle."

She tried not to flinch at his words. Hadn't she thought the same thing only moments ago? "That may be, Bishop Mueller, but I understand what I am getting with Abe Dienner. And my parents wished for the *kinder* to remain together, which is what Abe offers." She gave him a small smile all while biting the inside of her cheek. The whispers of her incompetence had met her ears on more than one occasion. Some in their community claimed at twenty-three she was too young to care for so many *kinder* on her own. Others ventured to mention the awkwardness of her gait, and now her limp was worsened by a foolish accident. No one mentioned how she'd failed to keep her younger sister Abigail safe when she ran out of the grocery and into the street. Only Naomi seemed to remember that fact, and the consequences of taking her eyes off the *kinder*. She'd been six, Abigail five. It didn't seem right that Abigail had died so young, or that Naomi had been responsible because of her disability. She forced the long-ago memory to the back of her mind and focused on what the bishop had said.

"The farm is a lot of work," he continued. "I understand Abe has experience with farming and is a *gut* farmer, but will he keep his word to you?"

Honestly, Naomi didn't know if Abe would or not, but he was offering hope. Something none of the others had given her.

"Farming is not something I am unaccustomed to, and Abe will set things right," she said, wondering if Abe had a farm in Haven that he was anxious to return to. "As I mentioned, I have accepted his offer," she said, leaving out the fact Abe intended on leaving.

"Don't forget, you must have the community's blessing as well as mine. Without it, there will be no marriage, especially given your *fater* is not here to give his approval. We only want what's best for you and the *kinder*, Naomi."

She sobered. Would the bishop approve of Abe? He had once before, but if he disagreed with the match, the community would follow his lead. "Bishop, if I don't hold it against Abe for leaving, neither should the community."

"I will take that into consideration." Bishop Mueller dipped his hand into his waistband and pulled out a packet of letters tied with a ribbon. "Three more letters from community members making their case for the *kinder*. In case you change your mind."

Hands shaking, Naomi took the letters from the bishop and placed them on the arm of her chair. The community had given their blessing to her and Abe once. Was that good enough or would they require a new blessing? It was not something she wished to think about. Not now when a glimmer of hope finally shone on them.

"I am concerned this offer has come from Abe Dienner." The bishop considered her for a moment. "He has not proven to be a man of his word and left you in a bind."

"The only trouble he caused was to my pride, Bishop

Mueller." She worried her hands together. "However, knowing Abe as I do, I cannot think ill of him. He must have had a good reason for leaving Garnett."

It was strange to her how her opinion of Abe changed when she came to his defense. Did she believe her own words? Truth was, she wasn't certain. She'd thought she knew Abe, but that all had changed when he'd left town.

"Even so, he should have told you, and because he didn't, I believe he has proven untrustworthy, Naomi."

"That should be my decision, ain't so?" She peered up at him. "My parents did not lay out guidelines for my choice of husband, only that I must marry."

The bishop pressed his paper-thin lips into a tight line. "They would not be pleased with Abe Dienner. I can assure you of that. He broke his word to you, and I caution you against such a match."

Taking a deep breath, Naomi said, "I beg to differ, Bishop Mueller. My *fater* was a man of quick forgiveness and grace. Neither he nor my *mamm* held any ill will toward Abe." She was immediately taken back to the moment when her parents sought to ease her broken heart. *Daed*'s hand firmly squeezed hers as *Mamm*'s head rested on her shoulder. The three of them sat beside each other on the sofa. "My *daed* asked me to carry a great deal of grace for Abe as the shoes he wore were perhaps not easy to walk in. I hadn't understood what he'd meant, not until I began walking my own path of difficulty after their deaths. My *daed* was wise, and I believe his advice and request sound. I will give Abe grace, and therefore, the benefit of doubt. Can you and the community stand by our beliefs and extend grace as well?"

Bishop Mueller pierced her with a hard, unyielding

gaze. Naomi's heart pounded against her chest. She'd carried Abe's previous rejection around like a basket of dirty laundry. Refusing to put it down. It wasn't until moments ago, when she'd spoken of her *daed*'s words that she'd realized the heaviness of carrying the heartache, and if she was going to ask the bishop and the community to give Abe grace, she had to do more than say she would. She would have to act on her words even if it went against every fiber of her being.

For the *kinder*'s sake.

Chapter Three

⟞⟋

Abe halted his footsteps the moment he saw the closed buggy. Fear clenched his chest, tightening at the thought that his *daed* had shown up at the Lambright farm unexpectedly. The moment he saw Bishop Mueller on the stairs talking to Naomi, he uncurled his fists. Had the bishop brought another marriage offer to her? One more appealing than his?

Although he didn't intend on sticking around, the thought of Naomi marrying another man didn't sit well with him, especially if they insisted on forcing her to give up the *kinder*.

A small hand slipped inside his, and he glanced down to find Daniel's toothless grin smiling up at him. Hannah worked a few feet away, clawing at the packed dirt with a hoe in preparation for the vegetable garden that would be planted later in the spring. In the last few hours, Abe had come to grow fond of Daniel. All the Lambright *kinder*, really. It was as if he'd never left town. But there was something about Daniel that pulled on Abe's heartstrings. The boy struggled to speak, and Abe wondered if he felt a kinship with him since he'd often struggled to find his own voice as a child, too. Not because he couldn't, but because fear had often kept him silent. But Daniel's silence didn't mean he wasn't intelligent. Abe saw it in the sparkle of the child's eyes when Abe instructed him on where the milk buckets went. Not to be outdone, Zeke jumped to his feet, dust swirling around them. "Nomi okay?"

Uncertain if the boy spoke of Naomi's fall from the ladder or the fact the bishop stood in the front yard, Abe nodded. "Yes, Naomi is okay."

"Nomi cry." Zeke's small voice pierced his chest and had him looking at Naomi from a distance. He didn't see any signs of tears, only irritation. Did she often cry after the bishop's visits? He ground his teeth together. He suspected her tears were from the decisions pressed upon her shoulders, decisions she wouldn't have had to make had he kept his word to her instead of leaving. Those tears could have been stopped if he'd married her like he'd promised. If only there had been another way he could have stayed and married her. But even if he could have, he wouldn't—couldn't—have married her and subjected her to the violence he'd seen inflicted on his own *mamm*.

Abe had kept the anger buried beneath the contentment he'd been expected to maintain. Until that night he encountered his *daed* pummeling Levi while *Mamm* cowered in a corner with her eyes bruised and swollen. Even now, the anger fueled into rage like a roaring wildfire. The violent reaction at yanking his *fater* off his *bruder* haunted Abe's sleepless nights. He knew in that moment, he wouldn't—*couldn't*—subject anyone to the darkness he'd grown up with, especially Naomi.

"No cry, Nomi," Zeke said, tugging on Abe's hand and bringing him back to the present.

"Should we see if Naomi is okay?" The boys grinned at him, and he swept Zeke onto his hip, grasped Daniel's hand a little tighter then strode across the yard. Abe stopped at the bottom of the stairs and set Zeke on his feet. The child scrambled up the stairs and tucked himself to Naomi's side. She readjusted her position on the chair and wrapped her arm around Zeke. The child smoothed his hand up and down her arm.

Something warm and soft bathed his aching heart at the child's attempt to comfort his older sister, but even more so at the softening of the lines that had marred Naomi's brow. If he'd had any doubts about marrying her so she could keep the *kinder*, they'd dissipated in that moment. She needed them and they her. Offering her a marriage in name only was the least he could do for the previous trouble he'd caused her. He knew of several married couples living in separate communities, so it wasn't unheard of among the Amish. Having grown up with a violent *daed*, he could understand the necessity of living apart. If only *Mamm* had had the courage to find refuge outside of his *fater's* shadow.

"*Gut* morning, Bishop Mueller," he said as he climbed the stairs and stood beside Naomi.

"Morning, Abe. It is *gut* to see you."

The tightness around the bishop's words made Abe wonder if he was being sincere. "Has Naomi shared the news with you?"

"*Ach, jah.*" The bishop's eyebrows furrowed together.

Abe sensed Naomi's immediate distress, and he dropped his hand to her shoulder.

"I can't say I'm pleased about the situation," Bishop Mueller said.

Heat raced to Abe's cheeks, but he cooled his ire. It would do no good for Naomi and the *kinder* if he let his temper get the best of him. "I understand your concerns, Bishop. However, rest assured I intend on keeping my word."

"The *gmay* believed you were a man of your word when you approached us for our blessing once before."

Abe's teeth gnashed together, but he forced himself to calm as he prayed for wisdom. "I agree I could have left town on better terms," he said, squeezing Naomi's shoulder. "At least, I could have given Naomi and her parents an explanation. However, my leaving couldn't be avoided."

When the bishop continued to look at him as if he'd grown two heads, Abe removed his hand from Naomi's shoulder and crossed his arms. "I did not leave the Amish community, Bishop Mueller. Only Garnett. My faith is strong, perhaps stronger since my departure."

That was the truth. He didn't blame *Gotte* for his *daed's* actions, but it was hard to keep the grudge against him from hardening his heart. His time away from Garnett had helped release him.

"And now?" Bishop Mueller asked.

Although uncertainty nipped at his heels, he didn't hesitate to answer, "My faith is strong."

"That is not what I meant. What are your intentions toward Naomi?"

"To abide by her marriage requirements, which are to keep the *kinder* together, here at their home."

He'd stay as long as he needed to get the farm back in working order, just as he'd told her, but then he'd leave—hopefully before the violence so prevalent in his family took hold of him again.

The bishop shifted his stance as he looked from Naomi to Abe then to his feet and back to Abe again. "You've not answered the question I wish to know."

A vice clenched around Abe's chest. "Then perhaps you should ask a more direct question."

"All right, then." The bishop pierced him with a hard look. "Do you intend on remaining in Garnett?"

"Bishop Mueller," Naomi said as she reached out and clasped Abe's hand. "I believe that should be between us, ain't so?"

"In most circumstances, I would agree, Naomi. However, with no immediate relatives, as your bishop, I believe it is my responsibility to see you in a suitable marriage."

"And you believe a suitable marriage for me would require me to give up the *kinder*? To separate my family?"

"A suitable marriage would be to one who honors you, Naomi. One who speaks his word and keeps it." The bishop crossed his arms and looked to his feet. "I fear Abe has proven to be untrustworthy."

Naomi released Abe's hand, and he immediately wished for the warmth and comfort of her touch back. She grasped the rail, and when he realized her intentions, he helped her to stand. Her actions made him stand straighter, taller. This woman—so small and seemingly fragile, filled with so much strength and courage—made him feel as if he could take on anything. Anyone. Even his *fater*. If he'd been anyone but Abe Dienner, he could be happy with Naomi and have a real marriage, but he was Abe Dienner, the son of a violent man, and he'd proven to carry the sins of his *fater*.

"It is I who must trust my future *mann*, ain't so?" she asked. "And when Abe tells me he had his reasons for leaving, reasons which aren't his own to speak of, I believe him."

Abe mentally rocked back on his heels at her defense of him. Too many times when he'd tried to do right on behalf of his *mamm*, she chastised him for his interference.

"He is the first man to ask me what my terms of marriage are before making his offer. That—" she paused and smiled up at Abe "—is honoring his future *fraa*. However we go on from here, Bishop Mueller, is up to us. Whether he stays or leaves once the farm is set to rights, that is up to us. I ask you to give us your blessing. If you do, then the community will, too."

A smile spread wide across his face at Naomi's words. Had anyone stood up for him the way she just did? If he were to ever marry for real, he'd be honored to have her at his side until death parted them.

"I am to understand, then, you don't intend on remaining in Garnett?"

Abe knew the duty of a *mann* was to provide for his *fraa* and family and to work hard. Once they were married, her siblings would become his responsibility. How could he keep his word and leave Garnett, as he told Naomi he would, and be the proper Amish husband he was expected to be. He swallowed hard, but nodded. "You don't have to worry. I will do my duty to Naomi and the *kinder*."

Somehow, someway, he would split his time between Garnett and Haven. One foot in both communities was the best compromise he could imagine. Naomi could have her marriage to save her family, and he could find his peace in Haven, far from his *fater* and the turmoil he wreaked. And he could keep his distance from the *fraa* he shouldn't have.

"And you don't intend on moving to Haven?"

Naomi's quick nod sent a jolt of uneasiness through him. He'd never thought of asking her to move to Haven with him. Still, he must remind himself he could never have a real marriage, one where he resided in the same dwelling with his *fraa*. He feared his temper and the actions that could follow if he became irritated with her or the *kinder*.

"I see," the bishop said, rubbing his thumb and finger over his beard. "It is not a good start for a marriage, but I realize any marriage offer Naomi would have accepted at this point would have been one of convenience. I see your offer, Abe, as no different. I will grant my blessing on one condition. Abe, you must remain in Garnett for three months after the wedding. That should give you plenty of time to set the farm as it should be and properly get to know your *fraa* and allow you both to make a well-thought-out decision."

Three months was much longer than three weeks. He swallowed the knot in his throat and felt it settle directly in the pit of his stomach. He could avoid his *daed* for a few weeks, but for three months? Was that possible? He had to try for Naomi's sake. He squeezed Naomi's hand. "What say you?"

She smiled sweetly at him, but he couldn't help noticing the hesitation in her normally bright blue eyes, and maybe a hint of fear. He didn't like seeing the fear he'd seen so often in *Mamm*'s eyes, and he wanted to do all he could to remove it, posthaste.

Bishop Mueller cleared his throat. "As much as I don't

like it, I can say that many couples have married for lesser reasons. At least the two of you know where you stand with each other. Naomi, I hope you understand what you are doing. I can see *lieb* for your siblings is guiding you—I just hope it isn't a decision you come to regret. A hasty marriage doesn't offer time for either party to break the agreement."

"If we are to marry by the will's stipulations, we can't wait until next fall for our ceremony," Abe said. The sooner they married, the sooner his three months would end and he could return to Haven. Far from his *fater* and the anger nipping at Abe's heels, waiting for him to explode and prove once again he was his *daed*'s son.

Shifting his weight, Abe removed his hat before settling it back on his head. The slight movement sent a breeze through his thick hair and gave him the push he needed to say what was on his mind. "Given the circumstances, and if Naomi is in agreement, we should be married as soon as possible."

The bishop pierced Naomi with a hard stare. "You're certain you're set on marrying Abe?"

Tension rolled from Abe's shoulders at her quick nod. He didn't know why her answer mattered so much to him, except that it was important she keep the *kinder*. He didn't want a *fraa*, and for all intents and purposes, he wasn't getting a real one but rather, one only in name before *Gotte* and the community. He owed her that much.

"We could have the wedding here, this Tuesday, if the *gmay* gives their blessing. I realize it is short notice, but I have no family outside the *kinder*. It would be a small ceremony. Our families only."

Abe shook his head. He had ruined her first wedding.

And he didn't want to deprive her of a true wedding day. "I have two requests. One, Naomi and her sisters be allowed to shed their mourning clothes for the ceremony. She will want to wear them until the year of mourning is complete, but for the ceremony, I ask that she wear what she chooses. And two, we gather as much of the community together and celebrate our union. Today, if at all possible. Tomorrow, at the latest. Naomi deserves a wedding, as all Amish girls have."

Naomi worried her bottom lip for a moment. "I don't wish to bother your *mamm* overly much. I'm certain she would want to do the things my *mamm* cannot, but I won't impose, especially on such short notice."

Her words pushed his heart into his throat. How had he forgotten the bishop would need to speak to his parents? Would *Daed* protest the wedding? If not, what would his *daed* require of him? During his time away from Garnett, Abe had come to realize how much his *fater* bullied and manipulated his sons and *fraa* to meet his own ends. If Abe wanted his blessing, no doubt, it would cost him, but what would that price be?

Late the next afternoon, after hours of preparation, nervousness shook Naomi's knees as she fought to keep her hands from trembling. A barrage of smells, from the grilled hot dogs to the pies warming in the oven to the various potato salads and slaws, clung heavily in the air, but for some reason vinegar infused her taste buds and coated her throat. She understood the need for a hasty wedding and was glad for it, but she had not expected it to be the day after she'd accepted Abe's proposal. She needed time to acclimate herself to the idea of becoming

Abe Dienner's *fraa*. If she weren't depending on this ceremony to keep all her siblings together, she'd leave and insist on more time. At least they hadn't married yesterday and she'd had the night to contemplate her decision.

"You should smile," Grace Beachy whispered over Naomi's shoulder. "It's a happy occasion, and you are a beautiful bride."

Naomi glanced at the girl she'd known since their school days and offered her a half smile. Next to her friend stood Ira, her husband of a few months. Theirs had been a love match. Ira had known since they were in the fifth grade he would marry Grace, and he had. Naomi envied them as their wedding had been a happy occasion. They loved each other deeply, and it shone in their eyes. Their constant smiles reflecting the deep affection they held for each other.

Naomi might have loved Abe at one time. And their marriage might have been a happy occasion two years ago, but now it was fraught with uncertainty and anxiousness. It would have been better had the bishop allowed Abe to leave in a few weeks instead of three months. Then she and the *kinder* could have gone on as they had these last months.

However, it was a small price to pay for the gift Abe offered. Still, Naomi was torn. Once the deacon declared them *mann* and *fraa*, she no longer had to worry over the *kinder*, and being able to remain in their home pleased her greatly. But she would have rather married for love, like her parents had. She wasn't marrying Abe for love or out of respect, but out of desperation, and yet she would promise to love him, and he would promise to love her. To make matters worse, they would make that promise in front of so many who had spoken about her behind her back, some even laughing at her when he'd chosen to leave town.

A hard knot clenched in the center of her stomach, and she thought she was going to be ill. The urge to flee as far and as fast as she could kicked in.

Had that been how Abe felt two years ago? Had he feared a future with her, then?

She glanced up at the man standing beside her, so tall and handsome. His curly brown hair, in dire need of a trim, curled against the edge of his wide-brim hat. A muscle ticked in the side of his bare jaw, and she tamped down the anxiousness in her belly. They were here together, in this moment, and he wouldn't abandon her this time until after their vows were spoken. Of that she was certain. She had to remember, theirs wasn't a real marriage, but one of convenience and necessity. At least for her. He didn't have to marry her. He could have left her to the dilemma of which man to marry to avoid losing all her siblings. But he didn't. Abe had swept in to return one of their milk cows and ended up offering her marriage. Yes, she would be forever grateful, but he wouldn't be staying.

Forgetting about her injured leg, she shifted her weight away from Abe and hissed. He wrapped his arm around her middle and pulled her closer to his side. His head bent close to her ear, and she could smell the hay from the barn and, well, the black licorice candy he'd been so fond of when they courted.

"Not much longer," he whispered. "Lean against me."

A chill chased the tinge of sadness down her nape. She wanted to keep her distance and sever the attraction she'd always felt toward him. She couldn't allow herself to want to hold his hand. She couldn't allow herself to long for him, not when they had determined they'd live separate lives from each other.

Deacon Yoder shuffled in front of them and peered over his wire-rimmed glasses. "Shall we begin?"

Abe nodded.

A disgruntled noise from behind them startled Naomi and caused Abe to flinch. She turned to find Abe's *daed* glaring with his arms crossed and his face set like flint. Cold, mean eyes found hers, and a shiver raced down her back. Had Abe's *daed* been the reason he'd called off their first marriage? Did he think a disabled woman wasn't good enough to be a *fraa* for his oldest son? Was that why Abe's *mamm* and *bruder* hadn't come today? Was that why Abe had left her?

Abe's fingers flexed against her waist as if to offer her support, and she felt the final threads of distrust she had for him begin to dissipate. He'd kept his word, even knowing there would be adversity. And she'd keep hers, both to him and to herself. He'd given her the best gift a groom could give his bride: the chance to keep her siblings together and keep their home.

"Do you promise Naomi that if she should become sick in body that you will care for her as is fitting for a proper Amish husband?"

"Yes."

"Do you promise Abe that if he should become sick in body that you will care for him as is suitable for an Amish wife to do?"

She licked her lips, knowing this promise would not

be a lie. If he ever needed her, she would move mountains to care for him as she should. "Yes."

"Now, do you promise together to come to love, forbear and have patience with each other, and not part from each other until *Gotte*'s will separates you by death?"

Naomi drew in a small, slow, trembling breath at Deacon Yoder's piercing gaze. Had Bishop Mueller told him they planned to part ways at the end of three months?

Not wanting to tell a lie, she drew her eyes closed and inhaled the scent of the delicious foods all around her. The rich, sweet shoofly pie began to permeate the house, taking over the aroma of the hot dogs left cooling on the grill outside. Her stomach rumbled, and although embarrassed by the loud grumbling, she was thankful for the laughter surrounding her as she considered how to make a promise she wasn't certain she could keep.

She felt the loss of his warmth on her back, but quickly found her hand squeezed in his. The fingers of his free hand touched the curve beneath her chin and lifted. She opened her eyes and blinked. Abe searched her eyes with his dark brown ones, and softly said, *"Jah."*

A tremor raced over her, and she couldn't help wondering what he meant by the simple word.

"Naomi, how do you answer?" Deacon Yoder asked.

She searched Abe's face. How could she make him choose to honor his word to her when it failed to please his *fater*? Neither choice was wrong. It was their way. However, if Abe's *daed* was against their marriage, it opposed the promises he made her.

His shoulders were stiff, and she couldn't help remembering how Abe had made it clear he didn't want a *fraa*.

Not just her, but any woman, and yet he was here sacrificing his own wishes, and possibly those of his *daed*.

Abe squeezed her hand again and encouraged her with a nod. But she was still uncertain she could make him choose between her and his *daed*, but then he mouthed, "For the children."

A field of butterflies took flight in her chest. Her legs wobbled, and for a small moment, she thought she'd faint. Was there a better man than the one standing before her? When he'd broken his word to her before, she'd wondered, but now he seemed bent on righting that wrong. All for the *kinder*. And for that, she would choose to love him. She had to since she would vow before *Gotte* and the community that she would. And, she would remind herself each morning when she woke, she would choose to love Abe.

Even after he left.

No matter who she married, she'd be required to make the same vow. *To love.* The thought wasn't nearly as daunting with any of her other suitors. Perhaps because the others didn't have the power to break her heart as Abe had already done once before, and this time she didn't have her parents to help her weather the storm. However, she would promise to love him as she did the *kinder*, nothing more.

And she'd make certain she kept her heart distant.

Chapter Four

Abe pushed his potato salad around with his fork, and contemplated the events of the day. The ceremony had gone off without his *fater* making his objections, and for that he was thankful. But now, sitting here next to his bride and sharing a meal with their guests, he couldn't help the fear of what was to come taking hold of his thoughts.

He glanced in the direction where his *daed* sat among the guests and found him hefting his tall, lithe frame from the bench seat he'd occupied in the open living room. His *daed* wove through the guests, his steps heavy enough against the hardwood floor to be heard over the hum of conversation. Abe waited for him to acknowledge him as he neared the kitchen door, but he didn't.

Abe hadn't been surprised by his *daed*'s attendance, or his mother's absence. Not after the way he'd parted ways with his family, but he had been surprised by his *fater*'s silence. Especially after *Daed* made it clear Abe wasn't to return home.

Dropping his fork, Abe crossed his arms.

The tips of Naomi's fingers brushed the fabric covering his arm, startling him from his thoughts. The soft lavender color of her dress suited her pale complexion much better than the stark black mourning clothes she'd worn. "You look lovely."

A soft pink shaded her cheeks, and she dipped her chin. "*Denki.* You've barely eaten a bite, Abe. Is everything all right?" Her eyes filled with concern.

"*Jah,*" he grunted more gruffly than he intended, as was evident by the frown lines marring her brow. "I'm sorry, Naomi. I only wonder why my *mamm* and Levi didn't come."

She shifted and nodded toward the door. "You should speak with him, ain't so?"

He rubbed his hand down his jaw. There were only two reasons *Mamm* and Levi wouldn't have come to his wedding, and neither reason sat well in his stomach. He grimaced and fisted his hands.

"I suppose." As much as he didn't want to leave Naomi's side, he leaned close and said, "Excuse me a moment."

"Of course," she said. Her gentle smile and the slight bob of her delicate chin gave him courage, but it also filled him with a sense of guilt at having bound her to someone like him. A man capable of the things his father had inflicted on him and his family was not what Naomi deserved.

"*Jah,*" he drew in a breath and rose from his seat. "I suppose I should speak with my *daed* before he leaves."

Abe navigated the tables and benches with half determination and half dread. He hadn't told his bride anything was amiss between him and his family, but she was smart and observant. However, if he had it his way, he would keep it from her, just as he'd kept it from the bishop and the deacons all through his childhood. He and his *bruder* had understood the consequences of any-one discovering their father's abuse. Although Abe no longer lived at home, those consequences would be dire, especially for his *mamm*.

Slipping out the door, Abe called out to his *daed* with a wave. His father glanced around the yard. Abe sup-posed he looked to see if anyone else was around, and then his father stalked toward him. His jaw set like the stone Abe had spent much of his youth unearthing at his father's command. "What is it you'd have to say?"

Abe felt the harshness of his tone as if he'd been back-handed across the jaw. He jolted to a halt and planted his feet. The man in him longing for rightness straight-ened his shoulders. But the child in him wanting his *fater*'s love and approval cowed. "*Denki* for coming to the wedding."

Henry Dienner thrust a finger in Abe's face. "You are an embarrassment to the Dienner name."

This was nothing new to Abe—he and his *bruder* had heard it often over the years—but it still stung and festered like a spider bite.

"Marrying that girl has only added more shame to our name. Your poor *mamm* is beside herself, fretting over what the *gmay* must think of her and the son she raised."

Abe didn't miss how his father placed blame on *Mamm*. It had always been that way. Once *Daed* knocked over a lantern and nearly burned their home down. *Mamm* hadn't been in the house, but out in the chicken coop gathering eggs, and yet it had been her fault. The bruises his father had left behind kept his mother from church services for over a month.

"How is she?" Abe found himself asking even though

his *fater* had just told him. However, he wanted to know she was well. Physically, at least. The emotional toll of being married to Henry Dienner had been clear to him long ago. He only prayed he was a better husband to Naomi and she would not suffer the same fate as *Mamm*. Leaving Garnett as soon as his three months was up would help ensure Naomi would survive their marriage. Surely, he could keep his anger under control that long.

"You lost that privilege when you interfered with my business and questioned my authority, boy."

That authority nearly killed Levi. "Very well." Abe dipped his head and moved to turn back toward the house. "Naomi and I thank you for coming."

"The only reason I came was because the bishop assured me you are set on going back to Haven, and he asked me to change your mind." The rise of his father's eyebrow wasn't a question to be answered but a demand. If Abe knew what was good for *Mamm* and Levi, he would leave. "I expect you have a mind of your own and won't listen to your father, anyhow, and I told the bishop as much."

Abe understood what his *daed* meant.

"Bishop Mueller has asked I remain for three months." He hoped mentioning the bishop's request would grant *Mamm* and Levi a reprieve from any consequences of Abe's actions.

"Then I suggest you go as soon as you've settled matters here, and do not cause your mother and I any more grief than you already have."

And there it was. The command to leave Garnett at the first opportunity. Abe's heart thundered in his throat as it had done in many confrontations with his *daed.* This time, he was a married man with a family of his own—*a family of his own!*—to love and protect. His heart beat harder, faster. Would he forever be at the mercy of his unjust father, even as a man, a married man?

"A *gut* Amish man honors his father and keeps his word. He does not raise a fist to his father."

His father's words twisted their point into his conscience. Abe wanted to say a *gut* Amish man didn't strike out in anger, but he held his tongue. Abe had always tried to please his *daed*, then Levi came along, and Abe set himself up as a scapegoat for his younger *bruder.* Still, *Daed* found ways and reasons to punish them both.

"You've done neither and have embarrassed our family, and now you've dragged this girl into your evil ways. You are a disgrace to the Dienner name."

Bowing his head, Abe prayed for patience and wisdom in his words. He'd learned long ago it did no good to defend himself. By the time he'd considered what to say and lifted his head, *Daed* was gone. Teeth set together and fists clenched, Abe spun on his heels. Barefoot children giggled as they ran through the yard, chasing chickens. A neighbor's Aussie mix dog, with one blue eye and one brown, barked after them. The festive meal he left on his plate must have cooled by now. The earthly smells of churned earth and decaying leaves blew across him on the evening fall breeze, dispelling the mouthwatering dishes prepared by the women who gathered to help celebrate his and Naomi's union. He caught sight of his bride, sweet, gentle Naomi, who didn't deserve the burdens Abe carried, leaning against the porch rail. The evening sunlight, easing down the horizon, reflected in the windows behind Naomi and illuminated the wayward honeyed strands springing from her *kapp*. As if he'd swallowed a lemon, his stomach soured. How much had she seen? Had she heard his *fater*'s criticism? He could not read her face in the shadows, but he couldn't help wondering if she'd agree with his *daed*.

When she moved to descend the stairs, he held up his hand and shook his head. He'd married her to help her family. If she had regrets and reservations, he didn't want to hear them right now. He was thankful when she turned away and hobbled inside the house.

Slumping, he stalked into the barn. Fresh hay teased his senses, right along with the fresh manure. He couldn't help but be pleased with Caleb for carrying out half the chores he had given him earlier in the day. He'd have to speak to him about the importance of cleaning the stalls before laying the fresh hay down. It would do no good if the livestock became sick from a lack of clean stalls. Abe plucked a shovel from the hook on the wall and opened an empty stall, normally occupied by one of the draft horses. Abe glanced around wondering where the old boy had gone. Had Stanley escaped? He strolled down the aisle, noting the state of each occupied stall until he found the big black horse in the last one. A fresh layer of hay cushioned his hooves. Abe choked on a half laugh and half snort. The boy obviously understood the importance of a clean stall, but instead of cleaning Stanley's normal quarters, Caleb had moved him to an empty one.

Fifteen minutes later, and with all the stalls mucked and freshly covered, Abe's pulse finally settled to a normal rate. His anger and frustration dissipated like the morning dew burned by the sun. The barn always had that effect on him. He knew he should get back to the marriage celebration and reassure Naomi that he intended on keeping his word. But the fear she'd side with his father on him being a disappointment kept him rooted to the barn like a carpenter bee building a nest.

Would she ask him to leave sooner than the three months? After all, if his own *daed* thought him a disappointment and requested his departure from town, wouldn't his *fraa* want to be rid of him as well? He rested against the gate leading out to the pasture. Forgetting about wearing his good church clothes, he sank onto the ground and tried sorting out the tumultuous thoughts crashing around in his head.

He'd spent the past two years trying to heal and figure out who he was without his *fater*'s voice in his head. The distance had brought peace between himself and *Gotte*. Or so he'd thought. Had his time in Haven been nothing more than make believe? A time where reality hung in the air like a hot-air balloon waiting for the wind to stir? Or was tonight *Gotte*'s way of telling him there was more road ahead of him in navigating the path of forgiveness and peace toward his father?

"*Gotte*, whatever it is, whatever I should do or wherever I should go, I ask You to illuminate the way ahead of me." Rose mooed from above his head and began nibbling on his hat. Pulling away, Abe pressed his lips together into a tight line and drew in an irritated breath. "It would have been better had I remained in Haven, ain't so, Rose?" he asked, glancing up at the cow.

Rose nudged the latch with her nose and pushed against Abe's back with a jolt.

"*Jah,*" he said as he stood and secured the latch. He

stroked his fingers down Rose's nose. "I suppose if *Gotte* can use a donkey to speak sense into a man, He can use a runaway milk cow to guide a man's step, ain't so?"

There was an unfairness to it all. Not to him, but to Levi, *Mamm* and to Naomi.

"It's too late to grow cold feet, *jah*?" His cousin Malachi Stoltzfuss stood framed by the open barn door, his thumbs hooked into his suspenders.

Pushing away from the gate, Abe eyed the plate in his cousin's outstretched hand.

"Your bride thought you should eat and sent a fresh plate."

They'd only been married a little over an hour, and she'd already become a caring *fraa*. But then, that was Naomi. Always putting others first. Shame filled him. She made a *wunderbar fraa*. He only wished she could have had a more deserving husband. "That was kind of her."

"Naomi is a kind woman." Malachi handed him the plate. "And thoughtful. You could have done worse for a bride."

But she couldn't have done worse for her husband. The thought came unbidden. *"Jah."*

Malachi stepped farther into the barn, his heavy boots stirring up the dirt. He emitted a low whistle. "There's a lot of work to be done."

"Hard to imagine what it probably looked like before Naomi's *daed*'s passing."

"A lot can happen in ten months, especially if there is no one with many years of wisdom and experience to work out the upkeep of a working farm." Fingering a loose hinge, Malachi said, "You're up for the challenge. Farming has always been in your blood."

His cousin's affirmation lightened the heaviness in Abe's chest, loosening the barbed hooks his father had sunk into him. "Thank you."

"Now, marriage, I'm not so certain."

Abe laughed. "This from a man who has avoided that institution."

Malachi huffed and crossed his arms. "It is not unheard of. I have no time for or want of a *fraa*. You, on the other hand, have abandoned your bride twice. At least this time you stayed for the ceremony."

Shame burned his cheeks.

Malachi shook his head. "No explanations or regrets, Abe. I know your *daed* is a hard man. Remember the summer I stayed with you?"

Nodding, Abe recalled the thrashing Malachi had received when a coyote had snatched one of the chickens when he'd failed to latch the gate properly. Malachi didn't suffer the worst of what *Daed* could give, but it was bad enough. It wasn't long after that Malachi and his *mamm* moved closer to town, and farther away from them.

"I suppose he does not approve."

Abe shook his head to deny Malachi's assumption. "It's me he does not approve of."

"Does it matter as long as *Gotte* does?"

And that was the question. Did *Gotte* approve of Abe? How could He when his decisions did not honor *Gotte*'s word? He kept his word and married Naomi, and by doing so, dishonored his father when he agreed to the bishop's condition. The entire situation left him feeling twisted. Abe shrugged.

"Do you intend on going back to Haven?"

Pressing his mouth into a firm line, Abe drew in a long breath. "My marriage to Naomi is one of convenience, for the sake of the *kinder*."

"You are a *gut* man, Abe."

Those words washed through him like a swollen creek, crashing against the banks and bouncing back into the treacherous flow. If he were a *gut* man, he never would have proposed to Naomi the first time. He never would have courted her. Then none of them would be in the predicament they were in. *Mamm* and Levi would be safe from his *fater*'s violent hand, and Naomi would be safe from him.

"Stay in Garnett with your bride. You'll find your way together." Malachi shrugged. "Isn't that what you promised each other before *Gotte* and the church?"

They had, but how could he tell his cousin his fears, that he'd become his father and would cause harm to Naomi or the *kinder*? Besides, he wouldn't break another promise, not to her.

Grim-faced and shoulders heavy, he said, "I suppose I should get back to my bride."

"Don't look like you're going to your death, man."

Abe's laughter ricocheted through the barn. "What am I to do with a *fraa* who has banned me from the house except for meals?"

Malachi slapped him on the back. "Court her, I suppose. You should be an old hat at that."

He had courted Naomi once before, when he was filled with the fanciful notion that he didn't carry the same violent tendencies as *Daed*. All that had changed the night he left Garnett. Now, the one thing he didn't want, a *fraa*, he had, and if he courted her as a husband should, she might think he wanted to stay and make their marriage real. That was the one thing he could not do. He knew how it would end; an image of his *mamm* cowering on the floor with her hands covering her head had him shuddering. He vowed to himself and *Gotte* right then and there that Naomi would never have cause to fear him. He only prayed he left town before he broke that vow and any situation that might entice the monster beneath the surface took over his emotions.

Dishes clattered, and Naomi slowly made her way to the sink, where she could easily ignore the pain searing in her ankle. She told herself it would take no time at all to wash them. She could stand for a short time. Besides, the sooner the tables were cleared and the dishes were done, the sooner her guests would leave, and then she could find her bed and rest from the taxing day. She couldn't believe it'd only been yesterday morning she'd woken with the pressing dilemma of which offer to accept, none of them being acceptable, only to find herself married this evening.

She ran water into the dish pan, added some cold water from the faucet until it was cool enough to dip her hands into and then stacked a load of dishes into the water. She lathered her mother's homemade lye soap into the knitted scrubby and began cleaning the silverware.

"You should sit down and rest your leg."

Naomi turned and smiled at Abe's aunt Esther. "I will rest soon enough."

"*Ach*, you're stubborn. As stubborn as your *mamm* was, as I recall." Esther took the plate from Naomi's hand and dipped it in the rinsing water before drying it. "She was a *gut* woman. You are a lot like her, Naomi."

"*Denki.*" A smile teased the corners of Naomi's mouth. It was nice to hear someone recall her mother. Sure, it brought memories and sadness, but it warmed her heart all the same. For once, she wasn't attempting to comfort her *brudres* and *schwesters* in their grief while hiding her own. "And thank you for preparing all of this."

Esther clucked. "No bother at all. My nephew wanted you to have a nice ceremony. I only wished his *mamm* would have made it. She's not been herself for some time, hiding herself in her room, so Abe's father tells me."

Before Naomi could ponder that statement, Esther nudged Naomi's side. "I can't say I'm surprised Abe did the right thing. Only wished he'd done it much sooner. He's such a good boy, and it was simple enough to gather items from the pantry. The pies were cooling on the windowsill when your *bruder* came by yesterday. News took over the community like a wild grass fire, you know."

She did know. She hadn't been surprised by the bishop's ability to gather so many of their church members on short notice. But it had surprised her to see the number of buggies pulling up the drive and people piling out with baskets of food in their hands for the wedding ceremony. Her wedding. Especially since so many people had kept their distance since the death of her parents. Certainly they showed up in the first days and weeks after, but soon the visits slowed until they stopped altogether.

She'd been thankful Abe had cleaned the yard a bit,

or she would have suffered more than a little embarrassment at the state of their home. It was also a good thing their deep scrubbing day had been the day before Abe's arrival, else the house would have been more than a little dusty. She took a plate from the dishwater and washed it before handing it to Esther. Naomi's attention focused out the window and on the flurry of children chasing each other, her brothers and sisters among them. It was nice to hear their laughter again and to have her home full of people. Although she was ready to sit down and prop her leg up, it was *wunderbar* to have the frowns of her siblings erased for a time. It was the best wedding gift she could have received. And she owed that all to Abe. "I appreciate all that was done."

"There is no better way to start a marriage than to have the community surrounding you. I wish there would have been more time to prepare, but I understand the circumstances didn't warrant it. He loved you, you know?"

Naomi jolted. She turned toward Esther, wondering who she meant. Before she was left wondering any longer, Esther said, "Your *daed*. He wanted you settled in a *gut* home with a *gut* man."

"I know," she said. She just wished he would have given her more time, or made it known in the will the children weren't to be separated. That would have saved her from a lot of anxious moments. "I can't say it was a pleasant process of finding a husband, but at least the *kinder* can stay with me at home now."

"Let's not forget about a *gut* man, too." Esther cackled until she began coughing. Naomi drew her hands from the dishwater and patted her on the back until Esther shuffled closer to the sink. She drew in a few gasps and then moistened her lips. "Excuse me, child. Sometimes my air gets ahead of me. I might be biased, but my nephew is as *gut* a man as any."

Naomi could argue, but even if he had caused her a great deal of embarrassment and heartache, he'd rescued her when it mattered the most. Still, his earlier abandonment left a lot of doubts about her worthiness to be any man's *fraa*. The fact Abe's *daed* seemed upset over the marriage and Abe's *mamm* hadn't attended the ceremony deepened those doubts. Did his *mamm* suffer from an illness that kept her confined to her room? Or was that just an excuse to keep her from her son's wedding because she didn't think Naomi was good enough for her son? The days and weeks after Abe left town, his *mamm* had ignored her when they'd gathered for church and when she'd seen her at the grocery store. Naomi had even tried to speak to her, but Martha Dienner had nearly fallen running from her. Naomi never tried to approach her again.

"Why am I not surprised to find you two on your feet when you should both be sitting?"

Startled, Naomi dropped a plate to the floor. It broke into three pieces. She gasped, and then gingerly kneeled, her ankle screaming as she did so. Abe crouched beside her. Their fingers brushed as they reached for the same broken piece. The spark of young attraction she'd felt during the early days of their courtship ignited something in her. She felt her eyes go wide and her cheeks flame. She jerked her hand back, and grabbing hold of the counter, she stood.

How was she going to make it three months with

Abe underfoot? Now that they were married, could she convince the bishop it would be wise for Abe to return to Haven at first light? Would Abe leave if she asked?

Abe gathered the pieces together and unfolded to his full height. He was much taller than she recalled and more imposing. "I'll finish up here. You two go sit down."

Naomi's nostrils flared at the command, and she was about to argue when Aunt Esther touched her forearm. "Come, Naomi, we should do as your husband asks."

Husband? They'd been married a little more than an hour, and he was already telling her what to do. She understood the ways of a *mann* and *fraa*, but they did not have a true marriage, which meant she didn't have to do as he said. Right?

"Naomi," he said, his voice soft. She barely heard him. "I don't wish you to cause further injury to your ankle. If you don't rest it, it'll take longer to heal."

His words did little to soothe her ire or unravel the confusion twisting her thoughts. "And what makes you a doctor?"

His handsome mouth curved into a smile. She'd spent hours staring at that wondrous face when they'd traveled in his open carriage during their courtship. She'd spent many more hours dreaming about him.

"It's common sense, Naomi. Besides, I've cared for livestock when they've stepped wrong. I know their care."

Did he just say she lacked sense and then compare her to *livestock*? She only lacked sense when she agreed to be his *fraa*. "*Jah!* I am a cow, now?" She crossed her arms and set her chin.

Aunt Esther cackled. Abe scowled.

"I'll leave you two to your spat," Esther said as she shuffled into the other room.

"You are not a cow, Naomi."

"What then, a pig? A goat?"

Abe scratched his head. "I was only giving an example of my experience."

"And comparing me to livestock."

"Naomi, please."

"No," she said, holding up her hand. "If I recall, we had an agreement that you would only step foot in the house during meals."

"It's our wedding celebration."

"Our guests are leaving as we speak."

"Then we should thank them for coming."

She scowled.

He threaded his fingers through hers and said, "Together."

She clenched her teeth together. She wanted to tell him she'd do it herself. After all, he'd spent the last hour absent from their table, leaving her to smile and nod with their guests as if all was right between them. However, the day had been long, and she didn't have any more fight left in her. She pulled her hand from his and immediately missed the calloused strength and comfort he offered.

"When the last buggy departs, you will go to the barn." She held his gaze, making sure he understood the rules for their marriage, and that she intended on keeping firm boundaries between them. Soon, he'd leave and go back to Haven, and she wouldn't allow him to give her cause to ask him to stay.

Chapter Five

Naomi opened her eyes and glanced around the small room. Her walls were pure white except for the year-old butterfly calendar *Mamm* had purchased before the accident and the blue curtains covering the window. A wardrobe, made by her *daed* from the prettiest cherry-wood sat in one corner, and a matching nightstand was nestled between her bedroom door and her single-sized four poster bed. She drew the quilt over her nose for warmth and drew in the scent of sandalwood and vanilla. She jerked upright, and a sharp pain seared through her inner ankle. Air hissed through her teeth until the discomfort eased and she could think about the unfamiliar quilt.

The quilt, a bold array of pinks, blues and purples, had been a gift from Abe's aunt Esther, a gift for a *fraa* and *mann* to share. Naomi had forgotten she'd brought it upstairs to see what it looked like in her colorless room. Exhausted from the past week, she must have fallen asleep with it while contemplating what a real marriage would be like with Abe.

An entire week of being Abe Dienner's *fraa* and trying to pretend like she wasn't a wife. She'd buried her-

self in chores, hoping to avoid him as much as possible.
Which did no good, since she constantly wondered what
her husband was doing and where he was. Anytime she
passed a window, she looked for him. Whenever she
was outside hanging clothes or gathering eggs, she listened for his voice as he spoke to the *kinder*. Whenever
he caught sight of her, he scowled, and she knew what
he was thinking. She should be sitting, resting her leg.
She rested it enough when she slept, or so she thought.
She reached down and touched her ankle. Although the
pain had subsided some, the swelling had not.

She sighed. Her ankle seemed no better. It didn't help
that the tendons in her leg had been tight and twisted
since childbirth. So any injury would take longer to heal.
To make matters worse, she stubbornly refused, as Abe
had said on multiple occasions, to rest her leg. There
was no time for idleness or injury, and there'd been no
point in telling him her chores wouldn't get done while
she rested. The household was big, and many of the less
pressing chores had waited for many months while she
tried to maintain the necessary ones. The *kinder* carried large burdens and she wouldn't ask her *brudres*
and *schwesters* to bear more than their share over a mis-
hap. Still, she thought the pain and swelling would have
lessened by now. Had she been wrong about not letting
them and Abe do more for her or about seeing the doctor? She recalled her *daed*'s dislike of the *Englischers'*
medicine. Still she couldn't help wondering if she would
have gone if her fear of being seen as weak didn't un-
settle her so much.

A rich aroma wafted through her door. She glanced
over her shoulder and realized the gray morning light

had already filtered through the pretty blue curtains hanging on her window. Panic surged through her mind. There would be no time for breakfast. Thankfully, it seemed Rachel had already gotten up and made coffee. She supposed it was a cold cereal and toast morning. Not the best start to a long day, but it was better than nothing.

She tried not to beat herself up too much over the fact she'd slept in. The excitement of being married last week and then hiding from Abe as much as possible prodded her to ignore her natural inclination to rise way before the sun. Using the same exercises she did whenever her foot bothered her, she rolled her foot in circles. She winced at the stiff swelling rebelling against the movement. A tear rolled down the side of her cheek, and she swiped it away in frustration. There was no time for pain. No time for tears, not when there was a household to wake and chores to do.

She eased into a sitting position and leaned against the headboard until the throb lessened and she felt composed enough to light the lantern. She needed to gather the eggs and milk the cows, not to mention she still needed to finish the laundry from yesterday. Rain had interrupted that weekly chore, which had given her a pleasant respite. She'd baked several loaves of bread and a few pies. Still, she'd seen the brown smudges marring a few of their dresses that she'd failed to get out last week. She wasn't sure how she'd missed them, though, since she'd spent a great deal of time scrubbing and rinsing and scrubbing some more. Not wanting Sara to become upset over the stains, Naomi scrubbed until her knuckles chapped. It seemed Sara became easily upset over the smallest things ever since the death of their parents, and Naomi wanted to make all the *kinder*'s lives as simple and worry free as possible. Naomi knew she couldn't replace their *mamm* but she could certainly try and provide them with clean clothes. Seeing that the stains remained disappointed Naomi, but she'd work them out today. Maybe she'd find a nice shady spot and prop her foot on a pillow while she worked. Certainly, Abe couldn't find fault with that. And she wouldn't ask the *kinder* to do any of it for her. They had enough to do when they weren't at school without adding her duties to their tasks, like feeding the goats, cutting vegetables for dinner, sweeping the floors and removing cobwebs from the corners, which seemed to be a never-ending battle.

Sliding out of bed, she reached for the black long-sleeved dress and jolted at the sight of the lavender one hanging beside it. She drew her fingers down the fabric and thought about her wedding ceremony. Abe had said she looked lovely, and his eyes seemed sincere when he'd spoken the words, but she'd tried to ignore them. She'd been scared. She didn't want to fall in love with him again and suffer another broken heart because he didn't want her.

Experiencing a broken heart once had been enough for her, and this time her *mamm* wouldn't be here to help her pick up the pieces. Still, she knew fighting her renewed feelings for Abe might be futile since she seemed to constantly remember the joy Abe's compliments had elicited during their courtship when he drove her home from the singings. She hadn't remembered those moments until their wedding day, and she wasn't sure she liked thinking about them again.

After a week of marriage, she still had a difficult time

believing it. She was married, not to Jacob Haver, who was nearly old enough to be her grandfather, but to Abe Dienner, a man she never thought she'd speak to again after he'd left Garnett the way he had. Her face burned at all the preparations and waste when they'd canceled their first wedding. He abandoned her, leaving the community with plenty to gossip about. She still cringed at some of the stories she'd heard, wondering if there'd been any truth to them.

All that did not matter now. Not when she was married. At least in the eyes of *Gotte* and the *gmay*.

And, for all intents and purposes, she was a *fraa*, and yet she wasn't one. Not a real one. They'd spent an entire week barely speaking, and they would never live in the same house or share the same room, or share the beautiful quilt his aunt Esther had made. His broadfall pants would never hang on a hook next to her dress. There would be no hand-holding or stolen kisses like she'd seen her parents do. She wouldn't have a *boppli* to fill her arms.

Would she have had a *boppli* of her own if she'd married any of the men who'd offered to marry her? She cringed at the thought.

The truth was, all the others were barely acquaintances. Abe had been much more, and acting as they had the last week, as if he was nothing more than a hired hand, didn't sit well with her. It caused an ache in her chest. One she wasn't ready to identify because her old feelings for Abe were teasing her heart, and it wasn't fair for her heart to want a love like her parents had with the man who'd quietly rejected her. Especially knowing he would leave again.

Was this how their marriage would continue? Near strangers who passed each other in the yard as they tended to chores or sat in silence while they shared meals together with the *kinder*.

Wasn't that what she wanted when she barred him from the house except during meals? No! She thought it was, but she didn't like it, not at all.

She drew the lavender dress down and buried her face in it and recalled how he'd looked at her with such wonder that it had stolen her breath. His tender care and support as they waited for the deacon to lead the ceremony still warmed her, and she wanted that back. He'd been thoughtful and attentive, and all that was *wunderbar*. Except for his bossiness, but she was beginning to think she could overlook that flaw of his.

If she did away with her mourning dress and wore this one to breakfast, would he look at her the way he had during their wedding ceremony? Would he speak to her beyond the monotonous daily list of chores needing to be done?

She sighed and dropped the dress to her bed. She'd set it in her mind they'd wear black an entire year. Her marriage would not change that, even if her union with Abe wasn't one of convenience. Still, she wanted to see him look at her like he had, as if she were pretty.

What did it matter? In less than three months, he'd be gone. Back to Haven and the life he had there. It was like reading a book and then losing it without ever knowing how it ended. A gnawing hunger for something more with Abe filled her, and she clutched her stomach against the discomfort. She knew it had to do with the loss of the friend she'd once had in Abe. Those days of friendship with Abe were nothing more than cotton fluff floating aimlessly about the sky, with no exact destination in mind. Some of the seeds would find the dirt and try to take root, only to be lost to the elements, while others would find hard, unforgiving surfaces and never see their seed planted.

The past for Abe and Naomi was hard and unforgiving. Too much time and hurt had filled the gaps between them, and she didn't know if the chasm could be bridged. The day of their wedding ceremony, she'd hesitantly trusted him, but she'd been desperate to save her family. He'd kept his word and given her his name, satisfying the terms of *Daed*'s will, but there had been little interaction between them to allow her trust in him to grow. And she'd been angered by the way he'd so easily stepped into his role of telling her what she should do the night of their ceremony. She'd spent days stewing over his high-handedness. Telling her to sit, and in front of his aunt Esther.

That had embarrassed her and irritated her, mainly because their marriage wasn't real. Just because she had his last name, it didn't give him the right to tell her what to do, even if it was for her own good. For sure and for certain, he only meant it for her well being. And the way her ankle continued to swell and cause her pain, she should be delighted at his intentions, but after dodging Bishop Mueller's persistent attempts at dictating who she should marry these last ten months, Naomi's natural reaction was to disregard anyone's advice, even if it was well intended. And since Abe would be gone soon enough, ignoring him made sense. So did being mad at him, which seemed to her a lot better than falling in love with him again. Was that wrong of her? Did it make her a horrible Amish *fraa*?

She slipped on her black mourning dress and kneeled beside her bed. Taking the small book of prayers from the side table, she stared at it blankly. The book had been helpful in guiding her faith this last year, but having memorized most of the prayers, she was certain there weren't any to help start her mornings as a *fraa* to a man who made it plain and clear he didn't want one. She sighed, and then she bowed her head.

"*Gotte*, I have no words, today. I know Your word says You're our refuge and strength, a help in our time of need. You have carried us through our grief, but I fear what the future holds. How can I trust my *mann* when he's broken his word before? I thought I could, but I don't know if I can."

She waited in silence for several long moments, not sure how or if she was ready to pray the next words. Knowing she'd made a vow before *Gotte* and the *gmay*, she knew she couldn't put it off. "As You guide us through our day, as You guide me through the day, help me love the man I call husband and keep my heart from the bitterness it so easily wants to cling to. Please, help me to love him without loving him. Help my heart to hold him while being free of him."

A creak on the stairs alerted her to the waking of her siblings. She'd wasted too much time already and needed to stir the coals in the furnace and then help Rachel with breakfast. She bobbed her head and said, "*Denki, Gotte.*"

Gingerly, she eased to her feet then looked in the mirror to pin her *kapp* better. She then slid her palms over the front of her ankle-length skirts. The scent of bacon suddenly tickled her nose. She listened for sounds in the kitchen. Had Rachel started breakfast, even knowing it was Naomi's morning to do so? Certainly, not. Rachel was difficult to wake up in the mornings, as were all the girls. Naomi opened the door and slipped into the hallway. The door to the girls' room remained closed. Naomi cracked it open and glanced at each of the four beds in the oversized room. She noticed the four lumps, one in each bed. Curiosity hastened her steps. She lit the lantern and pulled back Rachel's covers. "Girls, it is time to wake. Get dressed, say your prayers and get downstairs. Quickly now," she said with a clap of her hands.

Certainly, Caleb hadn't taken it upon himself to cook breakfast. The child didn't know how to light the stove, let alone crack an egg. She limped down the hall and opened the door to the boys' room. All three were gone. Even little Zeke, who was usually the last to rise.

Naomi slowly made her way down the stairs and tried not to be frustrated by the injury, which was keeping her from quickly investigating the kitchen. They'd only recently secured their home through her marriage to Abe; it wouldn't do to see it burned down by an overzealous, hungry boy of twelve.

She navigated the last step on the staircase and came to a halt as if she'd run into a wall. Abe wore one of the aprons that usually hung on a peg by the back door and stood near the stove. He flipped a few eggs onto a plate and then began cracking some more.

"What are you doing?"

"Good morning, my *fraa*." His smile beamed at her over his shoulder, giving her a look that turned her insides to Jell-O. She fisted her hands. True, she was his wife, but did he have to remind her of that fact? Especially after the confusing and convoluted prayer she'd just offered to *Gotte*.

"I hope you slept well."

She hadn't, but he didn't need to know that. She stalked toward the coffee and said, "Well enough. Why are you here?"

"I'm making my *fraa* breakfast on our anniversary."

"Anniversary?" Her brow scrunched together.

"How quickly my beautiful *fraa* forgets." He winked, and she feared her wobbly knees would give way, sending her to the floor. "One week of marriage to the loveliest woman I've ever known is worth celebrating."

She felt the heat of her anger. She couldn't—wouldn't—be taken in by his pretty words. "We agreed you wouldn't step foot in the house except for meals."

That was an agreement he'd kept so far, and she didn't want him breaking it now.

With his back to her, he flipped an egg and then another. "Yes, we did. Yet, I don't recall a time being mentioned. Since I am an early riser, and it is near six, I thought I would make breakfast."

The insinuation that she wasn't an early riser goaded her. She felt like she hadn't done her duty as a wife. "Men don't belong in the kitchen."

Ignoring her, he scooped the eggs onto a platter and carried them to the center of the table, next to a loaf of bread she'd baked yesterday. For the first time, she noticed the table had been set to perfection, just the way she would have. Daniel and Zeke sat at their places with their hands tucked into their laps. Waiting patiently. "If you'll call the girls down, I'll summon Caleb. The boy is milking."

Naomi's eyebrows shot up in disbelief. It took a lot of effort and convincing for her to get her *bruder* to help with the chores this early in the morning. She'd even noticed Abe had had a time of it this last week. "What did you promise him?"

Abe shrugged. "Nothing."

Shaking her head, she said, "I don't believe you. Caleb is a *gut* boy, but needs a lot of pushing to milk the cows." She sighed and then hollered upstairs for the girls to come down. "I'll see to it he has done it properly after breakfast."

"No need. I have confidence he'll do it correctly."

Footsteps clattered down the stairs, and one by one the girls entered the kitchen. None of them wore their dark-colored dresses. Naomi wanted to holler at them. They had attempted to discard their mourning clothes every day this past week. She couldn't believe their tenacity. Did they think they'd wear her down? Well, that wasn't happening, not yet, even if she didn't blame them for wanting to remove their mourning dresses. Hadn't she thought about doing that herself to see if Abe would look at her in awe again? It was *gut* she hadn't given in to the temptation since his compliments left her thoughts even more knotted than they had been before she came down to breakfast.

She pointed to the stairs. "Go back up and change. Our mourning time isn't over."

Their crestfallen faces tore at her heart, but it was the tears welling in Sara's eyes that nearly did her in.

"Listen to your sister," Abe said in a firm but gentle tone. "Hurry, before your breakfast gets cold."

Disbelief at their quick obedience to Abe's command spurred her irritation into a full-on gallop as the girls trudged upstairs. She glared at him. In less than a week, she'd lost control over her own home. And just as quickly, her attitude changed. Perhaps she'd never had control, given the amount of persuading she had to do throughout the day for her siblings to comply with the demands of a busy farm. Still, it rankled having him waltz into her home, change her name and gain the co-operation of her *schwesters* and *brudres* so quickly and easily when she'd spent months feeling like a hamster on a spinning wheel. Surely, it wouldn't last long. When he least expected it, her siblings would ambush him with rebellion, just as they'd done with her these last months.

"How's your ankle this morning?" he asked as he pulled out a chair and motioned for her to sit. Oh! They were back to this again. Why couldn't they ignore the fact that she was injured?

"Fine." She deliberately pulled out a different chair and plopped down onto the hard seat. The movement earned her a wince when she hit her leg against the table. Daniel banged his fork against the plate, his eyebrows raised high in question. Naomi made a shushing noise. "Patience, Daniel."

"Eat?" Zeke asked, speaking for his older brother, who'd rarely uttered a sound in his five years.

Daniel nodded and aggressively tapped his chin with his fingers. It was his attempt at signing *eat*.

"*Gut* job, Daniel, but no. You must be patient and wait for Caleb and your sisters, then you can eat."

The confounded man took it upon himself to sit beside her. He reached down, gently grabbed her leg and settled it on his lap, leaving the curve of her calf to rest nicely on his well-muscled thighs. This was something new. How had they gone from hardly talking to each other to him touching her? Instinct had her pulling away, but he held his hand firm. "I would like to see for myself."

Teeth gnashing together, she seethed. "When we said our vows last week, I thought we were to have a marriage in name only. You telling me what to do is overstepping."

"Only because you, my *liebling*, are stubborn," he said, flashing her a grin. Her insides hummed at his endearment, and she knew her cheeks turned strawberry pink as if she'd been outside in the heat of the day. "And you refuse to heed your body's limitations. Your foot is still bothering you."

She tried once again to pull away from his grasp, but he refused to budge. "I've had others telling me what I can and can't do. You have never been one of them."

As soon as the words were out of her mouth, she realized the root of her anger. Abe had never treated her differently than anyone else. He'd never treated her like she was incapable of doing anything. Was he doing so now because of her injury or because he'd decided she lacked ability?

"You've never been injured in my presence before."

Oh, why had she been foolish enough to attempt fixing the clothesline? If she hadn't, she wouldn't have fallen. Of course, that probably wouldn't have changed the fact she was now married. If she hadn't fallen and injured her leg, would Abe have stuck around and helped fix a few things around the farm? If not, her interfering siblings wouldn't have told Abe her troubles, and she would be married to Jacob Haver's *bruder* and settled somewhere in Missouri. Far from their home in Garnett. And without some of the *kinder*. Guilt cinched around her chest. She should be grateful for Abe's sacrifice to keep them together instead of being irritated over his concern for her.

The girls returned to the kitchen appropriately dressed and found their seats the same time as Caleb slammed through the screen door. A milk bucket weighed his arm down and milk sloshed over the edge as the screen door smacked against his back. Naomi inwardly groaned. Just another chore in need of tending.

"Eat," Zeke said once again.

"Not yet, little guy," Abe said. He then turned to Caleb and said, "Did you fix the clothesline?"

Caleb nodded. "*Jah*, again. That's once last week and once this week. It better hold this time."

"If you did it right, it will," Abe said.

"I did. Nothing will pull that line down."

"*Gut*, now set the pail on its hook and grab a cloth to clean up your spilled milk."

Naomi blinked at Abe's observation. She blinked several more times as Caleb did as he was told, but she was disappointed the distraction hadn't relieved her of Abe's hand on her leg. Soon she found her sock peeled from her foot. She prayed the shadows of the table would conceal the continued discoloring. Abe clucked faster and louder than the hens in the coop. "It's still black and blue."

"As expected, *jah*?"

His mouth formed a grim, flat line. "*Jah*, I suppose,

but usually not for this long. The swelling is much more than before. I don't think we have a choice but to see the doctor."

"No!" She jerked her leg from his lap and hissed. "I will not see a doctor. You know how my *daed* felt about doctors." Besides, she didn't want to be fussed over anymore than she already was, and she didn't want to feel like she was weak. "It will be well soon enough."

Caleb scraped his chair across the floor, the sound echoing in the large open room. The kitchen, dining room and living room was one wide open space, leaving very little to absorb sounds. Caleb began shoveling eggs onto his spoon when Abe reached across and stalled his hand in midair. "We pray first, *jah*? It is important to thank *Gotte* for the meal provided for us."

"You gathered the eggs, not *Gotte*," Caleb said.

She whipped her head in his direction. Her surprise and pleasure at the chore having already been done was overcome by Abe's piercing, hard look. She quickly glanced away. Did he think she'd shirked her duty in guiding the *kinder*? She had in many ways, especially when it came to praying before their meals. It didn't seem right to quiet the *kinder* before they ate if *Daed* wasn't here to say *Amen*. Even now, emotion clogged her throat at her good intentions gone wrong.

"As did you, Caleb. However, *Gotte* provided the hens to lay eggs for a *gut* breakfast, just as He provided milk from the cows." Shifting in his seat, Abe turned away from her and toward the table. "Now, let us close our eyes and bow our heads."

Silence muffled Naomi's ears and closed in the thoughts rolling through her mind. How had so much changed in so little time? What had she done by marrying Abe? She'd thought she'd gained her freedom, along with the ability to keep the *kinder* together and her home intact, but she was no longer so sure about her feedom. She waited with breath held for the one word that completely marked the end of the old and the beginning of the new. *Daed* had been the only man to lead them in prayer as a family at this table. Now Abe was stepping in as the head of their household. And although she was grateful for the opportunity to keep her siblings together, she wasn't certain she was pleased about the change, even if it was only temporary.

"Amen," Abe said, and before Naomi could collect her thoughts, silverware clanged against dishes, and just like that everyone acted as if Abe saying amen was as normal as breathing.

Abe didn't know how to go about his new role as husband, especially to a stubborn *fraa*. His only examples had been his father and Naomi's *daed*. The two men were as opposite as night and day, and when it came to their families, they were even more different. Abe recalled the firm yet gentle way Jeremiah Lambright had spoken with the *kinder* the few times he'd shared a meal with them. He didn't ask them to comply, they just did. And when Abe had taken to his bed of hay the last several nights in the barn, he knew he wanted to emulate Naomi's father. Not his.

He certainly didn't know how to guide young children who'd lost their father and mother. He imagined he should tread carefully with their tender, raw hearts. However, after seeing how hard Naomi had worked the past week, he knew she did more than her fair share around the farm while the *kinder* did as little as possible. He also knew he couldn't allow Caleb to continue with his idleness if he intended on leaving the farm in the boy's hands when he returned to Haven.

"The eggs are good, ain't so?" Rachel asked.

"Oh, *jah*," Hannah replied around a bite.

Caleb burped, smiled sheepishly and said, "Oops."

Zeke giggled, and Daniel grinned.

Abe tore off a piece of bread, and scooping some egg onto it, popped it into his mouth. He chanced a glance at Naomi for her approval, but she hadn't even taken a bite. Was her anger still piqued or did she have an aversion to eating food cooked by a man? When she noticed him staring, her cheeks flushed, and he felt his lips curve into a full smile. She was pretty. Very pretty, but she was even more so whenever her cheeks colored. It did not matter if they were flushed from the heat or from bashfulness or embarrassment, the color illuminated her blue eyes, making them glow.

"*Denki* for breakfast, Abe. It's *gut*," Sara said.

"You should not speak until your plates are clean," Naomi said, her eyes narrowing to mere slits.

Perusing her, Abe noticed the tenseness around her eyes and the grim set of her mouth. Was she still upset or in pain? She lifted her cup of coffee to her mouth, effectively hiding what he was looking for. He could only assume she was mad at him for *overstepping*, but from what he'd seen of her ankle, she had to be in a great deal of pain, too. Abe wasn't certain she'd only sprained her ankle. The discoloration of her skin pinched his stomach into knots, and he feared she'd broken something. But just as he had to find a way to guide the *kinder* with wisdom and a firm hand, he had to find a way past Naomi's stubbornness and anger. He'd hoped breakfast this morning would be a good start. He was tired of the silence between them.

"But, Naomi, we always talk," Sara said.

"Not when we have guests."

Her words were like a bucket of cold water over his head in the middle of winter. Not liking the idea of being no more than a guest in Naomi's home, Abe sat up straight and frowned. Sure, she'd banned him from the house except for meals, and their previous meals had been filled with awkward silence as if they didn't know each other's first names. And *jah*, he would leave at the end of three months, but he was her *mann*. Not a stranger. Not a guest, but her husband.

"Abe's not a guest," Caleb said.

Abe arched an eyebrow at Naomi and begged her to argue the point her *bruder* made.

"He's your *mann*, our new *bruder*, ain't so?" Annie asked innocently.

"Jah." Deep lines creased Naomi's brow as she reached for her coffee and sipped before settling it back onto the table. "But he won't be staying. You know that. Once the farm is in proper working order again, he'll leave. Less than three months."

The pleased tone of her voice grated on his conscience. It wasn't like he wanted to leave. He'd grown fond of the *kinder* as he renewed his connection with them. They were easy to like, as was their oldest sister, even with her prickly nature. No, he didn't want to leave. He *had* to.

The children all looked over at Rachel.

"Ouch," Rachel said after a rather loud thump under the table. She bent forward and rubbed her shin.

"Go on." Hannah nudged. "You said you would."

"Rachel, you promised," Sara added.

"I didn't promise." She scraped butter onto a piece of bread and brought it to her mouth.

"You did," Caleb said around a mouthful of food. "I heard you."

"What did you promise, Rachel?" Naomi looked at Abe. He shrugged his shoulders and almost felt the need to hold up his hands in mock surrender. The Lambright children had always been a force to be reckoned with, especially when they were all of one mind.

Rachel wrinkled her nose. "Oh, all right. Someone has to be the adult here, *jah*?"

"Rachel, don't be disrespectful," Naomi chastised her. "I'm your elder."

"So's Abe," Caleb said.

Denki, Caleb, Abe thought, wanting to give the boy a high five but thinking it was inappropriate to encourage him given the chastising looks coming from Naomi.

"Yes, Abe is your elder, and for the time being, I suppose he is considered the head of this household." Her shoulders slumped as if she was weary of arguing with the children. "I stand corrected. Rachel, do not disrespect *us*. Understand?"

"Well, if the cat is gray, should we call it yellow?" Sara snickered, eliciting laughter from Caleb.

"And what is that supposed to mean?" Naomi asked.

Hannah rolled her eyes. "You're not acting like adults, avoiding each other like you do and not speaking unless you have to."

"And, Naomi, I am sorry, but you wear a constant scowl on your face. Like you're always throwing a tantrum," Rachel said.

He couldn't help noticing how Naomi sighed then softened against her chair, losing the rigidness of her stiff spine.

"And, Abe, you're no better, hiding in the barn all the time. Which is why *they*," Rachel said, motioning to the older *kinder*, "have elected me as the adult."

When Abe came in to make breakfast, he hadn't expected any of this. Sure, he expected his wife to be as prickly as a locust tree, but he hadn't expected the storm brewing in the Lambright kitchen. Abe's head was already pounding with the fierceness of a three-pound hammer on a hedge post. His lack of sleep, due to the thoughts jumping around in his head, was making him anxious. He'd formulated a plan on how to fix all that needed fixing, but he still wasn't certain how to court his *fraa* without actually courting her. He wanted her to know she was special and he appreciated her courage and strength, but he didn't want feelings to get involved. He couldn't stay. No matter how much he wanted to.

If Naomi started acting like she could love him again, it would make it that much more difficult for him to go when the time came. Making her breakfast this morning had been a good start, or so he'd hoped. However, her reaction had been anything but pleasant. It'd probably be even less pleasant if she discovered the idea to make her breakfast had been born out of his own grumbling stomach. He'd been starving, and so he thought to make everyone breakfast.

"Let us hear what you have to say." Abe leaned back

against the spindle chair and sipped his black coffee. At the girl's hesitation, he said, "Go on, the day is running away from us."

"Well," she said, and then chewed her bottom lip. "We thought since you're married now you would stay."

Caleb snorted. "What she means is, you vowed to never part outside of death."

"You said it to the deacon," Annie chimed in.

"And wasn't that vow made to us, too?" Sara's darkening cheeks told him a tantrum was working up the pipes. "You didn't just marry Naomi—you did it for us. You promised not to leave."

"Sara," Naomi soothed. "It's not that simple."

Sara flew out of her chair, hands fisted on the table. "You always say that. Why can't it be simple?"

"Because Abe has his home elsewhere, and ours is here."

Sara turned her angry gaze to him. "Well, you can simply move back to Garnett and live here with us like a real family."

The pain in her words crowded the room, leaving Abe little space to think, let alone breathe. No doubt, her rash statement came from her grief, and he didn't know what to say to the girl, so he shrugged then shook his head. As Naomi had said, it wasn't that simple. He could never move back, not without his actions causing consequences for people he cared for and loved. When silence met her ears, Sara stormed out of the house.

Abe took another sip of his coffee and sensed many eyes upon him. He glanced around the table, avoiding making eye contact until he settled on Naomi. Deep sadness pooled in her eyes, and he knew this must have been a constant scenario since the death of their parents. Naomi had a big heart. She never could abide by others hurting. He imagined it was even more difficult for her when there was nothing she could do about it.

Clutching the table, Naomi moved to stand, but Abe held up his hand and said, "I will go after her."

"Uh, *jah*," Caleb said. "I wish you the best with that. She can be meaner than a two-headed rattlesnake."

"You shouldn't say such things about your sister," Naomi said, settling back in her chair.

"It's true," Hannah muttered, and Rachel nodded her head in agreement.

Annie held up her hands. "I'm not saying a word."

Naomi turned to Abe and pulled in a long breath. "I don't know if she'll respond to you, but *denki* all the same. Please, tread carefully with Sara. She's had a difficult time of it."

Clearing his throat, he said, "*Jah*, as I'm sure you all have."

If only he could turn back the clock and make different choices. He paused in his thoughts. Nothing would change. Nothing could change. It was only by *Gotte*'s grace he discovered the truth about his nature before he was supposed to have married Naomi the first time. They would have gone into their vows ignorant of the dangers lurking beneath the surfaces of his emotions. At least now, he made no promises to her outside of his name and setting the farm as it should be.

He left the table and pushed through the screen door into the crisp fall morning. With the rising sun behind the farmhouse, gray shadows clung to the yard, but it was easy enough to spot Sara on the rope swing dangling beneath the barren silver maple.

Pulling in a fortifying breath of air, he ambled toward her and prayed to *Gotte* for the right words to say to an eleven-year-old girl.

"I know I shouldn't tell you to go away," she said without looking at him, her bare toes digging into the loose soil as she swung back and forth. "But I'd like to be alone, if you don't mind."

"*Denki* for your honesty, Sara."

The child snapped her gaze at him. He took that as an invitation to sit on the ground beside the swing. He ran his fingers through what was left of the grass, wondering if he should say more or sit in silence with her for a while.

After several long minutes, she plopped beside him, and he felt warmth spread through his chest at the gesture.

"Nothing is the same."

He nodded. "Change is difficult. *Gotte*'s will is difficult."

"It doesn't seem fair," she sniffled.

"I know, Sara. A lot of times, it doesn't, but it is what it is." This he knew to be true. Life seemed unfair growing up, and at times mean, but he had to believe in *Gotte*'s wisdom and higher ways.

"I hate it."

"I know." He wrapped his arm around her small shoulders, and for a time, it was as if he was sitting beside Levi after they'd run from their *daed*'s fury. He missed his *bruder* deeply and longed to see him. However, his father's warning hung around him like a heavy chain. Abe wasn't certain trying to see him was a good idea, even from a distance. Abe hung his head. He didn't know how Levi felt about him. Each of the letters he'd sent to his brother had been returned unopened. Was Levi angry with him for leaving Garnett? It was obvious he'd tarnished many of his relationships. With his brother. With Naomi. He closed his eyes. How would he ever make amends? And for what was he to make amends? For leaving before he struck out in anger? And how was he supposed to help Naomi's little sister through her own anger and grief when he had yet to resolve his own? The thought of being cast out and barred from his family angered him even more. His father sought to isolate Abe from all those he cared for, and Abe didn't know what to do about it. He drew in a breath and considered his words carefully. "I know I haven't earned your sister's trust or yours, but please, Sara, if I could remain in Garnett, I would."

She looked up at him and swiped the sleeve of her dress across her nose and sniffled. "Do you have another family in Haven?"

He nearly laughed at that thought. His closest family resided here in Garnett. "*Nae*, truth be told, I live with my cousin and his dog. Neither of us can cook, and I sweep floors and stock shelves at the grocery store in town." He tweaked her nose. "I'd much rather milk cows and plow fields and listen to you argue with your siblings." And catch glimpses of Naomi while they did their chores. "I only have my *bruder*, *mamm* and *daed*."

"Then why can't you stay?" Her shoulders shuddered. "Why didn't your *mamm* come to the wedding?"

Her curious question, innocent as it was, pricked his

conscience. He didn't want to lie, but he wasn't sure he knew the truth either. "I don't know, Sara."

He dropped his arm from her shoulders and drew his knees into his chest. The sun behind him caught the tall grasses in the field like a river of gold. In the days before he'd left, Levi would sit beside him as the sun went down, chewing on a piece of wheat. He said it was like chewing gum. "If I knew why they didn't come, I'd tell you. And if I could tell you why I can't stay, I would, Sara. If I could tell your sister, I would, but I can't." Those secrets were deep and dark, and he feared the consequences should anyone find out about *Daed*'s abuse. "All I can do is keep the promise I made to Naomi. You must be content with remaining at the farm with your siblings."

"But I wanted a family again, like we had before *Mamm* and *Daed* died." Her tears rolled down the curve of her baby cheeks.

His heart ached for her, and he understood what she said. He wanted that for her. *He* wanted a family. But that wasn't possible, and he needed her to understand that even though her parents were gone from this earth, she still had a family. "You do have a family, Sara, it's just different. And you must know, when I return to Haven, I will come back whenever any of you need me, but I can only stay for a few months."

"My *mamm* wouldn't have missed Naomi's wedding."

Her low whisper cut him. And he didn't have a response. What could he say? His mother had been forbidden from coming? That she might have a black eye or worse? It didn't seem fair that Naomi's parents missed such an important event in their daughter's life and would miss all the rest of them with their children, when his own parents wouldn't celebrate the occasion.

"And if things still need fixing around here?" Sara asked.

The idea of staying longer than three months scared him for his *mamm* and Levi, and for himself as he didn't think he'd ever leave if he stayed longer. In the days since he'd returned, he remembered how much he cared for the Lambright *kinder* and their older sister. Their family had been so different from his, laughing and teasing and talking during meals. So loving. He'd spent every moment he could with the Lambrights while courting Naomi, always accepting invitations to meals. If things still needed to be cared for, he could hire someone to mend boards and fences, but that didn't sit right with him. Not when it was his responsibility. Anything that needed to be done needed to be taken care of by him. That was one part of his promise to himself he intended to keep. He just hoped he could do so without the consequences he feared.

"Then I suppose I'll stay until my job is complete."

Sara smiled up at him, her eyes intelligent and calculating, and he had a feeling he'd walked into a trap of some sort, but he wasn't sure what it was. He'd been victim to the Lambright children's pranks on more than one occasion while courting Naomi, and if he recalled correctly, Sara's smile was a precursor to her coming up with an idea she thought brilliant, but often bordered on a prank. He'd have to keep his eyes peeled wide-open and tread carefully, not to soothe the child's tender emotions, but to keep from getting caught in one of her tricks.

Holding up his hand for a high five, he asked, "Are we good, for now?"

"Oh, *jah*, very good." She smacked his hand and jumped to her feet. "Very good, Abe. *Denki!* But you should go see your *mamm*."

"I suppose I should." He'd been in Garnett for a week. It was time to go see her and Levi, or at least ride by and try to get a glimpse of them. That might be easier said than done, especially if he didn't want *Daed* to catch sight of him.

"My sisters and I will do your chores while you're gone." She took off running toward the house. Her words thundered in his chest. Sara wasn't the type to shirk her chores, but offering to do someone else's was suspicious. He'd have to speak to Naomi and let her know of his suspicions when they next met for a meal. He glanced up at the sun, knowing the noon meal was several hours away. A soft moo trickled across the field, and Abe wondered if Caleb had milked all the cows, and not just the one as he suspected. Since it was early enough, and he knew his *daed* would be deep in the fields before the sun got too high, he'd make sure all the cows had been tended to, and then he'd go see his *mamm*.

Chapter Six

Abe slowed the buggy as it rounded the corner. Fear and anxiousness stiffened his bearing, and the leather reins bit into his palms. He never thought he'd see this place again and had nearly forgotten many of the details of his childhood home, but nothing had changed. All remained as it had been, meticulous and in order. Just like his *daed* liked it. Abe scanned what was visible of *Daed*'s farm, searching the shadows of the porch for movement. Hints of life emanated from behind the fluttering curtains covering the windows, and he could detect the smell of black coffee and sweet oatmeal. A rooster crowed and he pulled his gaze to the chicken coop before searching the goat pen and finally the barn. The cacophony of the farm was much the same as Naomi's farm, except it wasn't nearly as loud, as if even the animals feared being heard.

The plow wasn't where it should be, and he couldn't see the old metal-rimmed tractor *Daed* used resting inside the barn. He turned his focus to the house. Was *Mamm* inside baking?

He pulled in a slow breath to better smell the distinct, tantalizing flavors of baked oatmeal and strong black coffee. A smile tugged his lips at the gentle hint, and he recalled the times he'd sat with *Mamm* and rolled dough with her. They were vague memories, but they were happy ones. He recalled his *grossmammi* singing a favorite hymn, and his *grossdaddi* always smiling and joyful as if he were the sun. But *Daed*? He had no early memories of him, and Abe didn't know why. He'd never thought about it before now. He'd never questioned those memories. Now he wondered. Why was his *fater* missing from parts of his childhood, and what had caused his father's anger? Abe pulled on the strands of those memories, like pulling barbed wire from years of overgrown grass and weeds, but nothing came. It was strange how he had early memories of his mother, but very few of his father.

A breeze blew around him, rippling the sleeves of his shirt. Tin slapped against tin, sounding like a rifle, and Abe near jumped out of his skin. He searched the yard and spied a loose corner of the roof rattling against the barn. *That* was unlike his father. Forcing the tension in his shoulders to loosen, Abe guided the buggy to the side of the road. He pulled the brake and rested his elbows on his thighs as he took another look around. Seeing nothing else out of place, Abe wondered if a recent storm had loosened the roof. Still, it seemed odd that it hadn't been fixed, given *Daed* always had him and Levi out to fix any damage once the rain stopped. Even though he'd planned to see *Mamm*, he hadn't intended going near the house. Fear continued to nip at his common sense, but curiosity overcame that common sense. Believing his *daed* was in the field, he could risk approaching the house. He jumped to the ground then hitched the buggy to an old hedge post. Careful not to be seen, he hugged the bare honeysuckle bushes lining the fence while keeping his attention focused on the house.

The line of giant silver maples hugged the blue sky with their bare branches, the effect almost ominous. The lack of leaves shimmering in the wind spoke of fall, even if the air was warmer than it should be. The trunks, however, beckoned him. They were large enough to hide his cousin Malachi, and his shoulders were broad enough he had to angle himself through most doorways. By the time they left elementary school, his cousin was nearly a foot taller than their classmates. *Mamm* once teased that Malachi drank too much cow's milk. Abe strode to the protection of the maples, pressed his shoulder into the bark and hooked his thumbs around his suspenders.

The screen door screamed open, and, hunched over, his *mamm* pushed through with a basket full of laundry. She descended the stairs sideways, one laborious, slow step at a time. Stark gray strands sprung from her *kapp*. She'd aged in the two years since he'd left. More than she should have for her forty-five years.

No sooner had she reached the barren patch of ground than Abe slid from the shadows and the basket fell from her trembling hands. She clasped one palm to her chest and glanced around wildly. Abe knew she was looking for his *fater*. She took a step forward, but Abe raised his hand to halt her. Sixty feet of dry patchy grass stood between them, but Abe felt the anguish and fear in his mother's eyes. He ran across the distance and touched *Mamm*'s pale cheek and then kneeled to gather the laundry basket and handed it to her. They stared at each other for long seconds. Fear beat against his chest. "I had to see you," he said. "You're well?"

"Well enough. Happy to see my *sohn*." She blinked a lone tear from her lashes. "You're married?"

Her voice was hoarse and gravelly.

"Jah."

"Your *daed* says you're not staying."

"I can't. *Daed*..." Abe scrubbed his hand down his jaw, the smell of hay and the leather reins tickling his senses to awareness. For the last week, he'd had purpose and drive. Working to bring Naomi's home back to proper working order had done that. Especially with all the unexpected problems like the runaway cows and wandering goats. Working at the store in Haven had propelled him into boredom and monotonous motions. He didn't feel at home in Haven. He didn't feel as if he could truly breathe. He was tired of hiding. He was tired of pretending as if nothing had been wrong growing up, as if their family was like all their neighbors in the Amish community. Happy and good. Even more, he was tired of being treated like an outcast by his own parents, as if he'd been completely in the wrong. *Jah*, he pulled his *fater* from Levi in anger and caused him injury, but he'd been trying to save his brother. Besides, didn't Scripture say fathers shouldn't provoke their *sohns*? He wouldn't pretend with his *mamm*, not when she lived it too. He could no longer keep quiet here. "I can't be him. I can't do to Naomi what he's done."

She knotted her hands together. Her complexion seemed to turn ashen gray. He reached out to touch her, this woman who had given birth to him and, at one time, had offered her sons open arms and ready laughter.

"I won't be the cause of anymore pain to you or Levi." He drew in a trembling breath. "I've done enough."

Her mouth quivered, and large tears clung to her dull blue eyes. "You're a *gut* boy. You always were."

Abe was taken aback by her words. Her mind seemed to drift off to another place and another time as she stared at the patchy grass. "This isn't the life I'd dreamed for you when I first held you in my arms."

He didn't know what to say. Certainly she'd seen warning signs of his *daed*'s abuse before she married him, but he wasn't one to judge and would not judge *Mamm* for a choice she made many years ago.

A smile touched his *mamm*'s mouth. Her eyes even held a glimmer of light. "You love her."

It wasn't a question, but a statement, and it hit him in the gut hard. He had loved Naomi once before, or thought he might. But love wasn't a luxury he could afford. He shook his head. "*Nae.* I can't."

Mamm considered him a moment and then nodded. A thousand questions raced through his mind, but not one landed long enough for him to ask it. Besides, the longer he stayed, the greater the chance his father would catch him. He turned to leave.

"*Nae*, Abe, please don't go."

Her plea pained him, and he jolted to a halt, but the noise of a tractor could be heard in the distance. He shook his head. *Mamm*'s eyes went wide, and he understood the fear quaking through her. He'd felt the same fear many times himself as he waited for punishment to be given.

Swiveling on his heel, he strode through the yard and tried not to harbor a bitter heart toward either of his parents. He couldn't remain in Garnett. It was *Gotte*'s will.

"*Ich lieba dich!*" His mother's words carried on the

breeze, creating a vice-like grip around his chest. Had she really said that, or had the words been a figment of his imagination? It had to have been the latter since he couldn't recall ever hearing those words from anyone but Naomi, and that had been several years ago. His mother's question burned in his thoughts. Did he love Naomi? *Jah*, he was sure he did, but it wasn't something he wanted to admit, not even to himself. All he knew was he enjoyed being around Naomi. She made him smile and laugh, and his heart seemed light and free of fear whenever he spent time with her and her family. Was that love?

The only other times he ever heard the word *love* was during the beatings he received.

A father's love doesn't spare the rod.

The memory of his *daed*'s words rocked through him, and he threw himself onto the buggy seat. If black eyes and broken bones meant love, he wanted nothing to do with it. He didn't want to receive it, and he most certainly did not want to give it. His heart had never been happy, then. Sad. Hurt. Angry. Those were not *gut* feelings, and he never wanted to feel them again or be the cause of them.

Which meant he needed to keep his barriers up. Keep to himself and as far from Naomi as possible. He would ignore Malachi's advice to court Naomi. He couldn't afford to be lured in by her kindness, and even more pressing, Naomi couldn't afford for him to be lured in and tempted to stay. It was good she prohibited him from coming into the house except for meals, but after this morning's meal, with the comradery and teasing, he'd wanted to linger, to be a part of that family Naomi's sister ached for. He wanted to sit at the table with Naomi and the *kinder*. That was a dangerous thing. A selfish one.

He would see that he no longer took meals in the house. He'd either request a plate be brought to him, or he'd live off peanut butter and jelly sandwiches. He could do that for three months. Stay far from Naomi and the *kinder*. Even though it went against his instincts. He'd only hurt them, and the thought of hurting them angered him. It made him despise himself. He never should have come back to Garnett.

He wheeled the buggy around, and slapping the reins over the horse's back, Abe raced down the dirt road, fleeing from the nightmares that had plagued him as a child. Fleeing from the man he feared he'd become.

Snagging the last of the clean shirts from the laundry basket, Naomi pinned it to the clothesline and stood back with a look of satisfaction and relief. Finally, this week's laundry was nearly complete. Even though she'd had to wash and hang it more than once, since the clothesline had broken more than once leaving the wet clothes to mingle with ground. Still, there was something satisfying about having one task completed on her list of things to do. Now, she could prepare the kitchen to do the one thing she loved to do more than any other: bake.

She bent over and picked up the woven basket before limping toward the mudroom, where she slipped off her shoes and pushed the basket onto the shelf. She collapsed onto the chair by the door and gingerly rubbed her ankle as she contemplated what she would do once the bread was rising.

Abe had seen to it that the *kinder* had done more than

their fair share. The cows were milked, the eggs gathered, the scattered buckets picked up from the yard and breakfast dishes put away. Thanks to Abe, who came back into the kitchen after consoling a temperamental eleven-year-old and washed dishes with said eleven-year-old.

Naomi shook her head. She'd tried to calm her sister Sara frequently ever since their parents' deaths. Rarely had her efforts worked, leaving Sara sulking for days, which had Naomi giving up trying at all.

Seeing Abe's results with Sara awed her. Of all the things Abe could have done to soothe the irritation she'd felt toward him since last night, witnessing his arm around Sara's shoulders as he tried to calm her was the last thing she'd expected. Seeing her sister's beaming smile melted her resolve to keep Abe from the house except for meals. She'd have to find ways to invite him in so he knew he was welcome. Her house was his now, as it should be with any *mann* and *fraa*. Except they weren't. They were pretending.

Naomi leaned her head against the wall and sighed. *Stupid, stupid, stupid.* She chastised herself for being such a silly girl. How did she ever think it was a good idea to marry Abe when they had a past together? A past filled with hurt and distrust.

As much as she intended to keep her distance from him, it would be nearly impossible, especially when her eyes continually sought him out. This morning he'd upset her, assuming her duty in the kitchen to make breakfast. His high-handed bossiness as he took her foot in his lap not only angered her, but it embarrassed her and made her feel weak. Helpless. Her whole life, her parents had tiptoed around her, giving her only the chores they thought she could handle. Others within their church did the same, not allowing her to play certain games with her friends when she was a child. Even now, the other women often guided Naomi to the sink, where she could remain stationary, rather than hobbling around and tripping over her own feet.

Abe had never been one of them, which made his treatment of her this morning even more irritating and intolerable.

"He treated me like a *boppli* this morning, *Gotte*," she whispered. "Is that how he sees me?" As if she were incapable of the simplest task of making breakfast. Was it because of her disability or her injury? Of course, she was thankful he went after Sara in her tantrum. Not because of the searing pain from her ankle to her knee when she tried to walk, but because for once she didn't have to set aside her own feelings to console the child.

It was nice to have someone come alongside and help parent a parentless child. And she was grateful. And she was even more grateful when she realized how quickly the walls of hurt and distrust crumbled at his ability to bring the *kinder* from chaos to order. His interaction with the *kinder* this morning had warmed her like hot chocolate after traipsing through below-freezing temperatures to gather eggs. His gentle care with the *kinder*, the very souls of her heart, was like a bonded thread securing two pieces of fabric together. After he'd left the kitchen to go after Sara, Naomi had pulled herself from the table and wandered to the kitchen window, telling herself it was for Sara's sake. To make sure he didn't hurt her feelings further, but that was a lie, and she knew it. Sara could hold her own and often left others reeling with her angry words. She wanted to watch Abe. She wanted to watch his bearing as he walked across the yard and memorize the set of his shoulders when he was about to do something uncomfortable. She wanted to imprint into her mind how his eyes sparkled whenever he teased her.

"Naomi!"

Sara's shriek, followed by the slamming screen door, yanked Naomi from her musings. She pushed to her feet and then settled her hand to her chest. "What's the matter, Sara?"

"What isn't the matter?" Sara rolled her eyes.

Drawing in a breath of patience, Naomi said, "I can't address the problem if you don't tell me what's wrong."

"Our clothes are on the ground. Again! Stained! Ruined!"

"What? How? Caleb fixed the clothesline again this morning."

"*Jah*, a fine mess he did."

"Where's Abe?"

"Home," Sara said, even as she shrugged.

"Home?" Rejection slammed in her stomach. The blood stopped flowing through her veins and her breath stopped. She thought she was going to be ill. Had Abe broken his promise to Bishop Mueller and returned to Haven already? She clenched her jaw. At least he'd waited until after they'd spoken their vows this time, but he could have done it before the tendrils of longing for something more than a marriage of convenience teased her into hope.

"*Jah*," Sara said. "He went to see his *mamm*."

"Oh." Relief washed over her as her pulse thundered

and her lungs worked to breathe evenly again. And why did it matter if he stayed or not? It wasn't as if she loved him. It wasn't as if his ability with Sara this morning had the same effect on her as a bouquet of wild flowers. *Ugh!* What propelled her to think about his weekly gifts back when he courted her during the summer when they were in full bloom? It wasn't like she'd kept any of them pressed inside a journal tucked under her mattress for safe keeping. She grimaced at the lie she told herself. But, honestly, she'd forgotten about the flowers and should have thrown them away a long time ago.

So, why did it matter if Abe stayed or left town? Because she wanted to trust him. Their marriage might not be real, but trust was still important. He said he'd stay three months, and as much as she didn't think he would, she wanted him to. For her own peace of mind, and to prove to the *gmay* and the bishop they were wrong about Abe. Her father had believed in Abe, even in the aftermath of his daughter's broken heart. She didn't know if she'd ever see the pieces whole and complete again, but holding on to her *daed*'s belief that Abe was *gut* somehow kept hope thriving in her head.

"Very well." Naomi snagged the basket and shoved through the door past her sister.

"Where are you going?" Sara's bare feet slapped down the cement steps.

"To do laundry," she snapped.

"No, I can do it."

"*Jah*, you can, but the wash is my chore today, and I'll not shirk my duties over a little hurt ankle."

A snort rumbled through her sister. "I guess you

didn't see the size of your foot. It's as big as a melon. And Abe told you to sit. Which you haven't."

Naomi stepped forward and hissed, and then turned toward her sister. "It's hard to sit and rest when there are things that need to be done. Now, help me to the clothesline."

"Naomi," Sara said, but didn't say another word when Naomi held up her hand.

"I'll go by myself if I have to, Sara."

"Can't you wait until Abe returns?"

Naomi narrowed her eyes. When she'd thought he'd left much sooner than intended, a realization dawned on her. Abe would leave. Maybe not today or tomorrow, but he would. "Abe won't always be here, Sara. We cannot depend on others when we're more than capable of doing things on our own."

"All right." Her sister shrugged, and they slowly navigated the rest of the yard. "You're as stubborn as Rose. Never doing what you should."

"What I should be doing is laundry."

Laundry she'd just washed and hung on the line. She wasn't one to complain too much, but she disliked having to redo a chore she'd already finished. Especially when there were so many other tasks that needed doing.

"You'd chew off your own leg if you felt the need," Sara said.

Naomi held her tongue. They moved across the yard as the smacking of the wind tangled their dresses around their legs. Once they neared the posts, Sara released Naomi's elbow and raced to the other side. Unable to bear too much weight on her own, especially with the fabric twisting around her legs, Naomi fell to her knees and then sat in the grass. Air hissed through her teeth as she drew in slow breaths until the pain lessened. For sure and for certain, she regretted leaving the house.

"Our clothes are covered in stains again!"

Sara snatched their clothes off the ground and tucked them against her side. Naomi felt her brow furrow but forced it to smooth. "I've *Mamm*'s recipe for removing stains."

Little Zeke ran across the yard and sat with his legs crisscrossed beside her.

"I cannot wear dirty dresses to school." Sara tossed the arm full of clothes to the ground and stomped her foot. "I just can't."

"Sara, all will be well. You'll see." It had to be. She could not fail her siblings. "It is good you have a few days off, *jah*?"

Sara crossed her arms and stomped the distance between them. Naomi tugged on her sister's hand and pulled her down next to Zeke. She needed a moment to rest her weariness and to wait for the throbbing in her leg to cease. "Let's lay here a moment, Sara. Let's find the sheep in the clouds."

"How?"

Naomi looked at her sister. The simple question gave her pause, as she didn't think Sara was asking how they were to look for sheep in the clouds. It'd been their favorite pastime on clear days after the chores were done. When her younger sister remained silent, Naomi spoke. "How what, Sara?"

"How can you get up every morning before the sun and carry on like our lives haven't changed?" Sara asked. "How can you look for pretend sheep in the sky when it is falling on our heads? How can you walk across the yard when your ankle is injured like it is?"

"It's *Gotte*'s will." She repeated the words she'd heard so many times in the last month.

Tears highlighted her sister's sky-blue eyes. "Do you believe that?"

Naomi halted a shrug before her actions told her sister she had doubts. In truth, she wasn't sure what she believed anymore, but anytime something befell one of their neighbors, that was the parroted response. It was embedded in their way of life. She had to believe it was *Gotte*'s will. It was what the bishop preached from the pulpit when accidents happened. She finally said, *"Ach, jah."*

There was no other answer.

"Naomi, I know it's disrespectful, but I want to stomp my feet and shake my fist. At *Gotte*."

Hadn't Naomi done that very thing after she'd tumbled from the ladder? It'd only been last week when she feared that it just might not be *Gotte*'s will that her siblings would remain together as a family. The idea of going about life alone without the *kinder* had been frightening to her. She needed them. They gave her a sense of purpose. They filled her heart to overflowing. Without them, without the farm, she didn't know who she was, but *Gotte* had clearly heard her heart. Maybe not in the way she wished he had, but he did answer the cry of her heart with Abe's timely arrival.

"I understand you're upset." Naomi hugged her sister's shoulder. "We all are, but being mad will help no one, and it certainly will not help our cause in keeping the farm running when Abe leaves. We need to do what we can and learn what we can before he leaves."

"How can you be unmoved?" Sara asked. "You have no emotion. You didn't cry when Abe broke off the wedding the first time."

Naomi felt those words cut deep. She couldn't tell Sara that she had cried. Many times. Not because Abe had left, but because he'd left without telling her why, and then she had to live with the fear he'd left her because he thought she was an unworthy helpmate. A woman who couldn't carry her weight when it came to sharing their duties as a *mann* and *fraa*.

"And I haven't seen you cry since *Mamm* and *Daed* died. And you didn't cry this morning, knowing Abe will soon leave and once again we won't have a family."

She had cried plenty after her parents died. Soaked her pillow from dusk to dawn and scrubbed at her tear-swollen eyes before she woke the young ones from their slumber. They needed a strong hand to help keep them together, not a woman prone to tears. As for Abe—well, she'd been so angry bitterness had taken root. She had to keep her tongue in check, even if her heart remained bitter like apple cider vinegar. "Abe made a choice to leave Garnett."

That, she believed, had not been *Gotte*'s will, rather Abe's own wishes. Had it been *Gotte*'s will he'd returned when he had? Or had that too been Abe's own choosing? She wished she knew how to separate the two and know which was which, although, when it came to it, did it really matter? After all, Abe had shown up and saved her family by marrying her. What did it matter if it was *Gotte*'s will or Abe's doing?

There was only one way to pull Sara from her ennui. "Well, there will be no meeting Rachel after her shift at the diner and shopping for new fabrics if we laze around and don't finish the chores."

Sara squealed and jumped to her feet. "Really, Naomi? But you can't go to town. Not with your foot so injured. How will you drive the buggy?"

"*Ach jah*, if we get our chores done, we will go," Naomi said as she thought about the details of how she'd climb into the buggy and endure the bumpy ride to town.

"What about your leg?" Sara asked.

"*Ach*, I'll be fine. Now help me to my feet."

Zeke scrambled up and pulled on Naomi's hand, while Sara pulled on the other. Naomi cried out in pain as heat tore through her leg.

"Nomi, okay?" Crouched beside her, Zeke shoved his little face close to hers and peered into her eyes.

"*Jah, jah*, I am fine." She gauged the distance between her and the clothesline pole. It was too far. "Sara, pull gently."

Once Naomi was upright, she hobbled on one foot until she found her balance against Sara's shoulder. She gingerly touched her foot to the grass and winced.

"You're hurt bad, ain't so? You should listen to Abe and keep your leg up," Sara said. "You can't take us to town like that."

Naomi drew in a hissing breath as she wobbled. She could not hide her pain from the *kinder*, and she wouldn't offer them more disappointment when they'd had so much already. Now that they could stay together as a family, she wanted to keep them smiling and not worrying about when the next storm would come. "Nothing more than a twist of the ankle. It's stiff, *jah*, but I'll be fine, Sara."

Sara hung her head. "*Nae*, we'll go when you are well enough."

Naomi admired her sister's sacrifice. "*Denki*, Sara. That is a grown-up thing to do, but I'll manage."

"Nomi, don't die," Zeke said, squeezing her fingers tight.

Her heart skittered. She loved Zeke's innocence. She loved that he wanted her to stay with them, but it saddened her he thought about it at the tender age of three. "*Nae*, I won't die, yet. I will stay here with you, Zeke."

"Naomi!" Hannah's *kapp* strings flew behind her as she ran across the open field and toward the gated fence. The youngest of the sisters, Annie, ran behind her. Panic colored the normally subdued twelve-year-old, and Naomi's heart thundered against her chest. She scanned the field for Caleb and Daniel but did not see them.

"What's happened?" Naomi released herself from Sara's support and hobbled forward on one foot, praying she did not fall. "Please, let Caleb and Daniel be all right."

They worked in tandem to meet Hannah halfway. Sara's arm wrapped around Naomi's waist while Zeke gripped her skirts. Naomi's leg burned like hot coals in the fire, and when she saw the old doghouse *Daed* had made, she motioned for Sara to take her there. She leaned against it and lifted her leg out in front of her.

"Naomi," Sara's voice quivered, and when Naomi looked into her fear-filled blue eyes, her heart ached.

"All will be fine, Sara," she said.

Sara's hands formed fists at her sides. "Quit saying

that! Nothing will be fine ever again. Not with *Mamm* and *Daed* gone. And Abe leaving again."

Sara took off toward the barn, just as Hannah stopped in front of her, and Naomi worried she went to find Abe, even though he had yet to return from visiting his *mamm*. Hannah bent over with her palms against her thighs and pulled in ragged breaths. Annie collapsed on the ground beside her, heaving gulps of air.

"What is it, Hannah? What has happened?"

"C-c-c-ows," she stuttered between her breaths.

Naomi blinked, confused by the word. From her reaction, something terrible had happened, and all Hannah could utter was *cows*! Abe had secured all the latches so Rose couldn't get out anymore. She was the only cow prone to escaping. "Cows? Where is Caleb? Is he okay? Daniel?"

Hannah unfolded herself and glanced up at the cloud-dotted sky. "Oh, *jah*."

"They're chasing the cows." Annie swung her hand in the air toward the road and then let it dramatically fall over her forehead.

The wrinkles in Naomi's brow deepened. "Why are they chasing our cows? They should be in the barn."

"Cows!" Zeke said.

"Yes, Zeke, cows." Naomi hobbled on her foot, trying to keep the toes on her sore one from touching the ground.

"Before an *Englischer*'s car hits them."

Naomi groaned and wished, not for the first time, that her sister knew how to share all the details, not just the ones she considered important. Moistening her lips, she prayed for patience. "Why would the cows get hit by a car?"

"Cows, Nomi!" Zeke tugged on her skirts and pointed toward the road.

There, in the road, in a chaotic cloud of dust, were their milk cows. If they didn't get them soon, they would head to town, and then everyone would see this fiasco and descend on the farm, once again, telling her it was impossible for her—a young, disabled woman—to run the farm. Worse, they'd blame Abe for his incompetence, and she couldn't allow that to happen. She glanced down at the faces peering up at her. They depended on her to keep them safe and their home well-kept, and she was miserably failing.

Where was Abe?

Abe slowed the buggy at the sight of Sara running in the road. He pulled close and halted the buggy. "What is the matter, Sara?"

She glared up at him with her arms crossed. "The cows are loose."

"Cows?" He'd fixed Rose's latch as well as the other ones that needed it. He couldn't figure out how they'd escaped. Not without some help. "All of them?"

"All of them."

"Where are they now?"

"Heading to town, I suppose," she said.

He scratched at his prickly jaw, the growth a reminder he was now a married man. "And my *fraa*?"

Sara snorted. "I guess you're asking about Naomi." At his nod, she continued. "She's not resting her leg, if that's what you mean."

Drawing in a sigh, he leaned his head back and stared

at the top of the buggy. "Too much to expect from my stubborn *fraa*, I imagine."

Another snort. "If you sit there all day asking me questions, she'll have the cows rounded up and back home before you have time to rescue her."

He wondered what Sara was up to, but she was right. He couldn't waste any more time. "Get in."

As soon as she was settled on the seat beside him, he snapped the reins. The Lambright home was less than two miles from the home he grew up in, but the distance seemed farther as his mind raced with various scenarios he'd find once he arrived. Air moved easier in his lungs as the large white farmhouse and the barns came into view.

Then he saw Naomi. The closer he got to her, the more he realized how pale she'd grown. Where her cheeks had been a rosy hue beneath the sun, now they were pale, and beads of perspiration trailed the curve of her jaw. Several of the *kinder* circled around her, the youngest, Zeke, springing off his toes as he pointed to the cloud of dust moving down the road. Away from the farm.

He stopped the buggy by the hitching post and headed toward Naomi. He shook his head at her pure stubbornness. "What are you thinking?"

She locked her jaw and lifted her chin a notch.

He wanted to scoop her into his arms, carry her back to the porch and demand she remain seated, but he knew by the look in her eye she already thought he was acting too bossy. But it served her well, especially when she didn't know what was good for her.

"Hannah, Annie and Sara, help your *schwester* to the

house. Make her sit with ice on her foot. Tie her down if you must."

Naomi gasped. The sisters laughed.

"I'll get the cows."

Fire darted from Naomi's eyes. She opened her mouth to argue, but at his raised brow, she clamped her lips closed. He thought of watching the four sisters to make sure they heeded his request, but if he was to gather the cows before they reached the highway, he had to move quickly. He'd deal with Naomi later, and he'd take her to the doctor just to prove he was a man of his word.

Jumping the fence, Abe took off running across the open field. The shortest distance between two points was a straight line, and if he timed it right, he'd be in front of the cows and guiding them back in no time. Of course, he hadn't counted on the *Englischer* car zooming in behind them, pushing them harder and farther than Abe could run. He pumped his arms and legs and vaulted over another fence. He was about to gain ground and pull in front of them when the herd swerved in tandem, like a flock of geese following their leader. The movement was so fluid it reminded him of the high grasses caressed by the wind before the spring burn. He jumped across the two-foot-wide ditch and landed on the gravel road. He sprinted forward and ran alongside the group until he came in front of them.

"Yah! Yah!" He waved his arms above his head. They stopped, and the dust settled around their hooves. He darted back across the ditch and snatched a handful of brome from the field lining the dirt road, and then held it out to one of the cows. Pulling back her full lips, she took the grass from his hand then bent to nibble on the feast lining the ditch. The others followed her lead, and Abe breathed a sigh of relief. At least they were calm and weren't running.

Caleb, wearing suspenders and a dark blue chambray shirt, raced toward him, waving his hat in the air. Skidding to a halt, the boy bent at the waist and heaved in gulps of air. He peered up at Abe from beneath the shadow of his hat. "Abe, thank *Gotte*. I tried to stop them, but they're faster than I thought. Something must have spooked them, *jah*?"

"Jah," he agreed, eyeing the boy with suspicion. "How'd they get out?"

"I'm not sure. I heard a loud noise in the barn. I went to investigate and found they were already gone."

Abe wasn't sure how that happened. He'd have to inspect the latches again and then ask the *kinder* questions later.

An *Englischer's* truck headed toward them, and Abe feared the cows would start running again, but the vehicle stopped a good distance away. Two men jumped out of the truck.

"You need some help?" one of them asked.

Abe shielded his eyes against the sun and was shocked at the sight of his *bruder*. His shock was quickly replaced with anxiousness. Had Levi forgiven him for leaving town? His brother had grown, and if he guessed correctly was much taller than their *daed*. His shoulders were wide, and he looked a lot like their cousin Malachi.

Abe shook his hand. *"Gut* to see you, Levi."

"G-g-g-gut to see you, too, *bruder,"* Levi said, his stutter less prominent than Abe remembered. His *bruder* pulled him into a tight embrace. "I heard you were in t-t-town.

This is my driver, Trevor Meinhardt." His brother motioned to the other man.

"Nice to meet you," Abe said, shaking Trevor's hand.

"You as well," Trevor said.

Levi pulled him into another hug. "Are you staying?"

Before he could answer Levi, the sound of a puttering tractor interrupted him.

"Oh, *gut*! It's my *schwesters*," Caleb cried out.

Trevor laughed. "Sure can't get over your tractors. Not many Amish allow them."

"Glad our community does," Abe said.

The modern convenience was one Abe appreciated on the farm, and it was nice to give the horse and buggy a rest and motor to town on the big tractor. However, Caleb's declaration knotted Abe's stomach. Was Naomi on that tractor, too?

"Yep," Levi agreed. "Too many acres to work the land with our horses, especially in the heat of summer."

"Well, looks like you have your hands full. Anything I can do?" Trevor asked. "I have some rope in the back of my truck."

"Denki," Abe said as Trevor strode to the truck.

As the tractor came closer, Abe knew without a doubt Naomi wasn't driving, but she sure wasn't sitting on the front porch, either. There was no mistaking the stubborn tilt of Naomi Lambright's chin. Naomi *Dienner*, he reminded himself.

His cheeks burned with frustration. He fisted his hands at his sides.

"Trouble in marriage, already, I see," Levi said as he elbowed Abe.

Abe shook his head. "Nothing but."

Levi smiled. "Still, glad you married her. It wasn't right she became anyone else's bride, you know?"

"*Jah*, I know." Still, she was proving to be difficult, and he had a feeling her feathers weren't nearly as easy to smooth as her sister's had been. *Breathe, Abe*, he told himself several times as he approached his stubborn *fraa*.

"You're supposed to be on the porch with your leg propped up."

"You are not—" she said, and then stopped, turning her mouth into a scowl.

Even though she didn't complete her thought, he knew what she wanted to say, that he wasn't her *mann*. Her words held a bite of hurt and anger. Two potent emotions he was more than familiar with. Those feelings were why it had taken him so long to return home. Forgiveness was their way, withholding it was not. Still, he struggled with releasing the hold his father had on him after all the abuse he'd inflicted—not on him, he could have endured the punishments, but seeing his *mamm* cowering beneath his *daed*'s fist and Levi's broken arm had been too much. He glanced at his brother and wondered if he'd suffered too much in his absence. His *bruder* seemed cheerful, teasing and smiling. Not like a man who continually suffered beatings at the hands of their angry father, nor a man who hadn't forgiven him. Then he turned back to Naomi. What would it take to earn her forgiveness? He wouldn't blame Naomi for her attitude toward him. Couldn't blame her. He wronged her. But her refusal to be rational about her health only cost her. And frustrated him.

"Naomi, I am your husband in the eyes of *Gotte* and

the church." At the darkening of her cheeks, he rushed on to say, "More so, I am your friend, ain't so?"

He couldn't help noticing the panic in her eyes, but he tried to ignore it. "If you insist on causing further harm to your ankle, there is nothing I can do about it except take you to the doctor, but you must know, the more you refuse to rest your leg, the longer it will take to heal. I'm simply looking out for your well-being."

"And I suppose it was my well-being you were looking out for when you abandoned me before our first wedding?"

"Jah." The word was out before he could take it back. Whether or not she believed him, his leaving had been for her benefit, but he couldn't give explanations. She would believe him. Or she wouldn't. "We should get the cows back to the barn."

"Wait!" Naomi scooted off her perch on the tractor and looked around. Deep lines carved into her brow. Her jaw clenched, and Abe knew she was fighting the pain in her ankle. "Where's Daniel?"

Caleb slapped the flat of his palm to his forehead. "I left him under the big oak in the field. He couldn't keep up."

"By himself?"

Caleb gaped at her as if she'd grown two heads. "The cows—"

"Would have been fine. Now Daniel is by himself. Alone, with no way to get help if he needs it." Holding on to the tractor, she spun around as if to gather her bearings.

Abe touched her shoulder. "It will be all right. He'll be okay. We'll find him."

He recognized the worry in her eyes. He'd seen it several times whenever Levi had run off after a beating and *Mamm* couldn't find him. He dropped his hand from her shoulder and swallowed the lump in his throat when tears formed against the edge of her lashes. Fear mingled with trust, and he prayed he didn't let her down.

"Here's the rope." Trevor returned, handing the length of rope to Levi. "I gotta go, though. Some emergency on the jobsite. Levi, you know how to contact me when you need me to come get you."

"Thanks, will do," Levi said, waving to his driver.

"Levi, will you help Caleb and Sara return the cows?" asked Abe.

"Of course," Levi responded.

When Sara began to protest, Abe held up his hand. "Don't argue. We need help, and this is part of being a family." He wasn't sure of his own words about being a family since his wasn't a good example, but he knew how much it meant to the child to have a family again. "Hannah, will you take Naomi back to the house on the tractor?"

Naomi shifted, her scowl dark and threatening. He shook his head and hoped she didn't question him in front of the *kinder*. They may not be his siblings or his *kinder*, but it was his responsibility to help Naomi guide them. If she questioned him in front of them, they might ignore any guidance he offered. He scrubbed his hand over his jaw. "Please, Naomi," he said, "I will find Daniel and bring him home."

"What about me?"

At the tug of his sleeve, Abe glanced down and found Annie, the youngest of the sisters, staring up at him.

Remnants of breakfast clung to the corners of her mouth. He smiled at her and thought for a moment about how close Daniel and Annie seemed to be. This morning at the table, he'd noted how she dished seconds onto his plate and poured his milk. Maybe she could help him find the boy. "Would you like to help me search for Daniel?"

Chapter Seven

Naomi was unaccustomed to being told what to do by anyone but her parents. It didn't sit well with her. Quietly heeding Abe's wishes didn't sit well with her either. Especially when Daniel was missing. However, something stopped her from arguing with him, and she was certain it was the advice her mother had given her before she was supposed to marry Abe two years ago pressed into her conscience. *Pick and choose your battles and don't ever question him in front of the children. Save your arguments for behind closed doors.*

The myriad of emotions flitting across Abe's face had told her he was as uncertain about his role as a husband as she was being a wife, and he was maybe even more uncertain about how to proceed with the *kinder*. Her mother's words washed away the anxiety and fear she'd experienced in the last half hour, like she'd been caught in a torrential rainstorm. The wayward cows, worry over what the community would think about Abe's shortcomings and Daniel's disappearance. Gone. What mattered was supporting Abe.

If they were to get along the best they could as a family, she needed to quiet the hurt she felt over his previous rejection and forgive him. She'd have to stop dwelling on what might have been and focus on what was now. Yes, Abe might have broken her trust and her heart, but he was here now. And that was what mattered.

Chewing on the inside of her cheek, she glanced around at her siblings, each of them ready to complete the tasks given to them but waiting for her acquiescence. The part of her that had spent so much time making uncertain decisions on her own wanted to take control and argue against Abe's sound commands. She wanted to find Daniel herself. That part of her worried over Daniel. If something happened to him, his cries for help would go unheard. The thought of him wandering alone frightened her, but then she recalled he wasn't prone to wandering. If Caleb told him to stay put somewhere, he would stay. And she had to trust that Abe would find her little brother and bring him home.

She had to trust that he would do all in his ability to find Daniel.

"Annie will be a *gut* help, *jah*?" She hoped Abe understood the ground she was giving him, and she prayed the *kinder* would heed their direction without too much rebellion. "And, Sara, you've a way with the cows. We need your help—*I* need your help, and this is another grown-up thing to do."

The muscles in her shoulders released their tension the moment Sara's scowl dissipated. Naomi would have to find a way to make good on her word to take Sara shopping for new fabrics. "*Denki*, Sara," she said.

Naomi shifted her weight and stumbled sideways. Abe was there, wrapping his arm around her waist. He tugged her closer, encouraging her to lean on him for support, his scent dancing with the tendrils of her hair that had escaped from her *kapp* and grazed her jaw. A field of butterflies took flight in her belly. She pressed her palm to her midsection and drew in a few slow breaths.

"Are you okay?" he asked with his head bent close to her ear so no one else could hear. His consideration of her sent another field of butterflies into flight. How could she tell him that he was the one who unsettled her?

Once she found her voice, she said, "*Jah*, I am well. Just worried is all."

"*Denki* for supporting me with the *kinder*. I know they've had a rough time, and they'll find their way, but they won't do it if we do everything for them."

She considered his words. Had she been doing that since her parents' death? She remembered the months of exhaustion, trying to keep up with chores and farming. Which included milking, mucking stalls, gathering eggs, laundry, baking and scrubbing. She often told herself they needed the time to grieve. She wanted to make things better for them, easier. She couldn't find fault with Abe's observation though and needed to consider his words more.

"I will find him, Naomi," he said, squeezing her hand.

"I know," she said, sensing Abe needed to know she believed him, that she trusted him. At least in this. "Daniel will be at the oak. He wouldn't have gone off if Caleb told him to stay."

He nodded, helped her onto the bench her *daed* had made for the back of the tractor and then walked away without another word. Although, she wasn't certain what she'd expected him to say or wanted him to say. There was nothing more to say at the moment. Daniel needed to be found, the cows returned and, whether she wanted to admit it or not, she needed to rest her leg as the pain was becoming more and more unbearable.

She straightened her dark black skirts with trembling hands. Abe's touch had warmed her, his closeness had shaken her. The scent of hay and licorice remained with her, and she couldn't shake it. His scent continued to tease her senses and play with the memories of their courting days. She didn't like the memories. The feel of his warm touch against hers. His hip brushing hers as they rode home from singings.

She'd wanted to remain by his side, to feel his strength and comfort, and that wasn't good if she was going to guard her heart from him. Yet, she'd spent several long months playing mother and father to orphaned children by herself. She'd chased Rose whenever she'd escaped, hoping she'd catch her before she made it to town and proving Naomi wasn't capable of running the farm and managing the *kinder*. Not to mention everything else needing to be done that overwhelmed her, and then the things she couldn't do but was too ashamed to ask for help with, like fixing the roof. Seeking help always meant a lecture on choosing a husband.

Having Abe here, now, had been more than a relief. For once, since the deaths of her parents, she didn't feel alone. She didn't feel like a burden. And the thought of him leaving scared her. More than it should, especially after only having him here for a week.

The tractor rumbled to life, and Hannah drove it to the intersection at the end of the road to turn around and follow the cows pushed by Levi, Caleb and Sara. Naomi closed her eyes and drew in a deep breath. She tried to replace Abe's unique scent with the musky smells from the heavy woods lining the road and the cow droppings squashed beneath the tractor tires, but it wasn't working. She kept smelling him as if he still stood beside her. Which made her eyes flow with tears.

Surely, she was just overly happy and beyond grateful at having one problem solved. Last night, she'd gone to bed exhausted and wondering how and if they could have a real marriage. Tonight, it wouldn't matter, she would lay her head on her pillow knowing the *kinder* would remain in their home and Abe would do all he could to keep them safe.

Of all the men she could have agreed to marry, Abe was the only one who showed compassion and kindness while correcting them. He was the only one she trusted to have their best interests in mind. He'd make a *wunderbar* father.

Her stomach lurched at that thought. She had to be content with her life, no matter what came.

She had three months to acclimatize herself to his leaving, but she knew she'd have to get used to his constant presence here first and figure out how to go about as a married couple without being a married couple. For sure and for certain, once she did, he'd be gone.

"Ow!" Naomi cried as her leg swung against the side when they hit a bump. She gripped the edge of the seat, and the tractor jarred sharply to the right, then to the left, as they rode over a rut before settling back into a smooth cadence. She turned on the seat and rested her leg across the bench. She took in the various colors of the fields. She hadn't even inspected their fields to see if they had been cut or if they were overgrown with weeds.

Would they have a crop come spring or would they have to burn? There'd been so much to do and so little of her to do it. The early spring days were meant to prod hope into the hearts of man, but hers had been heavy with grief. Dare she hope, now?

Naomi believed the seasons were *Gotte*'s way of reminding man of his earthly duties. Summer was a time for toiling and tending, fall was for harvest and storing, winter for resting and renewing the mind with much time spent praying and reading the Bible, and spring was a time for shedding grievances and offering forgiveness where needed. It was a time for hope. And after many months of grief and uncertainty, she was glad for winter coming upon them to rest and renew her mind with prayer and *Gotte*'s word.

Once they were in the yard, Levi approached and helped her down from the tractor. "*Denki* for bringing the cows back." she said.

"No, *denki*," he continued at her raised eyebrow, "for bringing my brother back. I knew if anyone could do it, you could. I just hope he stays."

Swallowing hard, she wasn't certain how to answer since she didn't want to douse Levi's hopes. *"Jah."*

As soon as she said the word, she knew she wanted Abe to stay, not just for three months, but for longer. In the time he'd been here, her life had been easier. And as much as she denied it, the love she'd once felt for him stirred deep in her heart. But how could she convince him to stay when he was so set on leaving?

The moment Abe saw Daniel's little feet waving back and forth as he sat in front of the tree a wave of relief washed over him. "Come, Annie, I'll race you."

The little girl giggled and took off running before he even finished speaking. They ran the short distance, but Abe allowed Annie to take the lead so she could win. She collapsed on the ground beside Daniel and worked her fingers to communicate to him. Once she was done, Daniel nodded and jumped to his feet. Abe pressed his palm against the tree and pulled his hat from his head. "You're fast, *jah*?"

"I can beat Sara and Caleb, too."

"Well, shall we get back to the house before Naomi comes looking for us?"

Daniel tucked his hand into Abe's, and they walked through the field until they could see the peaks of the barns. "Want to race, again?"

"What about Daniel? He's slow," Annie said.

The little boy's face fell, and Abe felt his disappointment to his toes, even though Annie hadn't meant anything bad by it.

Abe swung the boy onto his back. "We'll see about that," he said as he ran over the tall grasses.

"Hey, *nae* fair," Annie cried as she sprinted behind him. Deliberately, he slowed his pace to give Annie a fighting chance, but as they approached the yard, Abe spun Daniel to the front of him, and as they closed the distance to the porch, he said, "Stretch your arms out, Daniel, and touch the porch. Let's win."

Daniel giggled, and Abe collapsed onto the middle stairs. A delicious smell filtered through the open windows and permeated the air. His mouth watered and his stomach grumbled in agreement. Daniel poked Abe in the chest and smiled wide.

"Oh, you think to tickle me, do you?" he asked as he began tickling the little boy.

Annie plopped down beside him, heaving air into her lungs. "You cheated."

"No, we won fair and square, didn't we, Daniel?" Abe said as he continued tickling the giggling child. "We won."

"W-wh-wh-on," Daniel uttered.

Annie gripped Abe's forearm, her fingers digging into his flesh.

"Yes, we did. We beat the fastest seven-year-old in all of Garnett."

"Wh-won-won." Daniel wiggled away from him and clattered down the stairs into the barren grass. He danced around in circles, his hands raised in the air as he jumped, singing his little tune. "Wh-won."

"Abe," Annie called his name, and he glanced down at her, just as the screen door slammed against the frame, startling him. He jerked around. Naomi's palm pressed against her chest, her mouth agape as tears streamed down her face. He jumped to his feet and climbed the stairs. He touched her arm. "Are you okay?"

"Yes, of course." Her gaze flitted from him to her younger brother. "I'm happy Daniel is home."

Abe dropped his hand from her and smiled. "I'm sorry. We should have come right in to let you know we were back, but we were celebrating our win." At her questioning brow, he said, "We beat Annie in a race."

"Daniel talked." Annie's little voice cut through the air as if it wasn't an everyday thing. Of course, Abe hadn't heard him speak since his return, but he couldn't recall Daniel speaking much before he'd left Garnett.

But Daniel had been little and spent much of his time in the house with Naomi's *mamm*.

"I know. He's never done that, not like that." Tears filled Naomi's eyes, and she sat on the porch furniture. She reached her arms toward Daniel and embraced him when he responded. "That was *wunderbar*, Daniel! Very *wunderbar*."

"Wh-on, wh-wh-on," he stuttered.

The brilliance of Naomi's smile warmed Abe, and he thought he would do just about anything to see her smile like that every day for the rest of his life. He watched her for a moment as she stroked the child's thick brown curls and kissed his forehead. The love she displayed for the *kinder* told him he'd made the right decision to marry her. He wondered if she would love her own *boppli* as fiercely as she did her *brudres* and *schwesters*. A vise clenched around his chest. When he'd offered to marry her in name only, he never considered what she would sacrifice. When the children were grown and gone, would she regret becoming his *fraa*?

She took Daniel's little face in her palms and kissed his forehead. "*Ich lieba dich*, Daniel. You're a *gut* boy."

Her softly spoken words, the same ones his own *mamm* had spoken earlier, cut him. He believed Naomi spoke the truth. Sincerity carved the corners of her eyes and colored the tone of her voice. He tried to recall how *Mamm* had spoken the words to him earlier in the morning, but all he recalled was the roaring of his hot blood.

He pushed the memory aside and focused on the celebratory moment. "It was a *gut* race, *jah*? Annie was close on our heels."

"*Denki* for bringing him home," she said. "I hope

you'll join us for lunch. I know we had a good breakfast thanks to you, but I'm preparing a casserole. Lots of meat and cheese and green beans, as I recall you liked it when *Mamm* made it."

His taste buds awakened, and he nearly jumped at the offer, but he needed to put some distance between them. He needed to go to the barn and work until all he thought about were the things that needed to be fixed before he left. And he needed to stay as far from Naomi as possible. He needed to quit thinking about her cooking. To quit thinking about her altogether and all the things he could never have with her. Like family meals in the house. He'd make a trip to the store to get some bread, peanut butter and jelly the next time he went to town.

"It smells *wunderbar*, Naomi." He glanced over his shoulder toward the milk barn. "There's a lot to do. I should help see to the cows. If you don't mind, maybe for dinner?" A flicker of doubt flashed through her eyes, and he rushed on to say, "I don't think any of us want to chase cows again anytime soon."

"Oh, *jah*, of course." Her small pink lips curved into an understanding smile. "I thank you for all you're doing. We've kept you on your toes since your arrival. I want you to know we—*I*—appreciate all you're doing. I know it's not easy."

"I'm doing nothing more than what I've promised, Naomi," he said, knowing his word couldn't be easy for her to trust.

"Please ask Levi to stay for dinner, too. There is plenty. It's *gut* to see him again."

Again? What had Naomi meant by that? Had she not

seen his *bruder* since Abe had left Garnett? He intended on finding out. *"Denki."*

He found Levi, Caleb, Sara and Hannah in the barn, where they were checking the latches on the gates leading in and out of the barn and out into the fields.

His brother gaped at one sixteen-foot red gate, dividing the pasture from the yard, with another connecting gate leading into the barn. He'd never thought about the abundance of gates on the farm, but he counted five just in his view and knew there were more on the other side of the barn, too.

"What's wrong?" Abe asked.

"Can't figure out how all these cows opened their own gates, and then the main gates. It's not like they have thumbs," Levi said.

Caleb doubled over in laughter.

"No, they don't." Abe's brow creased together. There had been no rhyme or reason for the great cow escape, unless Caleb had been careless in closing the gates after the milking this morning. He'd have to speak to the boy, but he'd wait until they were alone so he didn't embarrass him, and it'd give Abe a little time to consider his words. "Naomi has asked you to stay for dinner."

"Oh," Levi said, rubbing his stomach. "That would be *gut*."

"She asked about lunch, but I told her there was work to be done , but I see the cows are back in their places." He only hoped they'd stay put. Caleb began to run for the house, but Abe said, "Not so fast, young man. I hear we have a stubborn clothesline to fix."

"Awww, do I have to?" He wrinkled his nose in disgust. "I already did it once."

Abe raised an eyebrow. "And how many times have the clothes fallen to the ground?"

Shrugging, Caleb dug his bare toes into the dirt of the barn floor. His cheeks reddened beneath the brim of his hat, and Abe rested his hand on his shoulders. "Three times now. But I fixed it."

"Part of being a man is considering others more than yourself, Caleb. Even when times are hard. I realize you're young, but circumstances have asked you to act like a man. I'm not saying you can't have your fun and do things you like, but your family should come first. Your *schwester* is too humble to ask for help." That was a truth he'd known about her for years. She liked to do things on her own, stubbornly so, but sometimes it was to her own detriment. Like climbing the ladder to fix the clothesline. Abe was certain it had more to do with her need to feel competent, and less to do with pride. "I wouldn't want her to fall again and hurt herself."

"I'm sorry, Abe."

"No need to apologize, but we need to do better, and we'll do it together."

"Denki." Caleb said.

"I noticed one of the fence posts came loose," Levi said. "I'll see if I can fix it and check some others while I'm at it."

"Thank you, Levi, and after dinner, I would like it if we could talk."

He wanted to know where his *bruder* had been and why it seemed Naomi hadn't seen him for a long time, but more importantly, he wanted to ask his brother's forgiveness for leaving like he had. If Levi could forgive him, then maybe there was hope for Abe after all. Maybe he wasn't as big of a disgrace as his *daed* claimed.

"*Jah*, I would like that," Levi said. "Come along, girls. I'll show you how to know when a post needs shoring, and then show you how to do it."

Abe watched his brother and three of Naomi's sisters as they strolled out of the barn. He turned to Caleb. "Let's grab some new line, a hammer and some nails."

After they loaded up the ancient wooden toolbox, they began walking toward the house.

"Abe, may I ask a question?"

He glanced at the boy. "Yes, of course."

"I did a good job, fixing the clothesline." He motioned toward the line with his chin. "I know I did, 'cause I wanted to impress my friends who came to the wedding last week. Why did it break?"

"Well, we'll have to see. Could be the line is old and worn. But you know what, Caleb? I wondered the same thing about the milk cows. I know I fixed their latches so even Rose couldn't escape, and yet they all did. How do you think that is possible?"

"I milked them this morning and made sure to close the gates when I put them back in their stalls."

Listening to the boy, he was thankful Caleb broached the subject since Abe disliked confrontation. He knew Caleb needed guidance and correction when it was necessary, as all the *kinder* did, but he didn't want to assume Caleb had shirked his duties and accuse the boy, especially if he was innocent. "Are you certain?"

With an enthusiastic nod, Caleb said, "I even put the pins in the hasps like you had. You did good. *Daed* would have been impressed."

Emotion knotted in his throat at Caleb's words. Jeremiah Lambright had always been kind and patient with his *kinder*, never shouting or lifting a hand to them, but Abe had never seen them give their father cause to be angry. Still, the thought that Naomi's *daed* might have approved of something Abe did made him happy.

"Not even Rose could have pulled the pins. Like your *bruder* said, she doesn't have thumbs. Unless someone pulled it for her."

Abe stopped in his tracks and looked back to the barn. Had someone opened the gates intentionally? He scrunched up his brow and rubbed his palm over his stubbly jaw. "Do you think? Who? Why?"

"I don't know," Caleb said, shrugging. "I was joking. I don't think anyone did it, but it seems weird it happened."

It did seem weird, and he wasn't too certain Caleb was wrong. In fact, the more he thought about it, the more he was sure Caleb's observation was right. But who would have done it? Caleb was the obvious answer, given his age and his tendency for idleness when it came to work. Was this the boy's way of dealing with his grief? Recalling Caleb's wish to show off his work to his friends, Abe didn't think he'd sabotage something he'd fixed with his own hands and quickly disregarded Caleb as the culprit.

Which left the Lambright sisters, but which one? And why?

Chapter Eight

～

Naomi watched the pendulum wall clock as Hannah laid the dishes out on the table. "Don't forget Levi will join us."

"*Jah*, as many times as you've reminded me, you'd think you'd married him and not his *bruder*."

"Don't be a goose, Hannah. I'm just *naerfich* is all."

"I don't understand why. He's just a *buwe*," Hannah said.

"No, he's not. He's Abe's *bruder*." She sensed there was something more than a rift in Abe's family, and she wanted to return the kindness he'd shown her and the *kinder* by trying to fix things for him. Since Levi was here, she believed things between the *brudres* would mend much more easily than whatever lay between Abe and his *daed*. Naomi had a feeling she couldn't fix that, especially if he didn't approve of her as his son's wife. "Besides, I want Abe to like the meal. It's *Mamm*'s recipe that he liked so much. I haven't made it before without her—" she said, pushing back the memories of her mother bustling around the kitchen as she prepared large meals for her offspring. *Mamm* liked cooking and baking. She liked serving her family and always did it with a happy heart. Naomi believed that was always her secret ingredient, which she had yet to discover. Maybe because she worried too much about doing it right now that *Mamm* wasn't here to guide her. Naomi had been cooking and preparing meals for as long as she could remember, but she felt her dishes lacked the deliciousness her *mamm* provided. Was that because she often hid behind her mother's successes?

"Abe will love the meal," Hannah said.

Naomi hoped so since she wanted to entice Abe into the house for more than meals. She wanted him to feel welcomed and well-fed. He had to be well-fed if she was going to succeed in convincing him to stay.

The screen door squeaked open, and Naomi got to her feet. Caleb's bare feet slapped against the hardwood floors. He was followed by Annie and Sara. Then Levi, taller than his older *bruder*, ducked through the doorway and hung his hat on a hook by the door. "Abe said to start without him. One of the horses threw a shoe."

"Oh, *denki*." Naomi tried to keep the disappointment from her voice, but she knew by the apologetic look Levi gave her it didn't work. She sank back onto the chair and folded her hands into her lap. She wanted to be understanding, but she'd worked so hard for his approval. Couldn't the horse wait until after Abe ate? Was this an excuse to avoid her?

"It's *gut* Abe noticed it," Levi said, taking an empty chair beside Caleb. "A damaged hoof can complicate matters."

She chewed her bottom lip, feeling shameful at her self-pity. "I suppose it is *gut*. *Daed* took care of those things. It isn't something I know about. Would you mind leading us in prayer?" she asked, looking at him before bowing her head.

They sat in silence for several long seconds, but her thoughts were not focused on *Gotte* and her thankfulness for the bounty provided for them. Instead, her thoughts were solely on Abe and how much she really wanted him to eat her cooking. If she had something to offer him in exchange for all he was doing around the farm, maybe, just maybe, he might stay in Garnett longer than his three months, but he never made it to the table.

Two days later, Naomi slipped outside with a book and a linen towel full of ice. She hobbled toward her favorite spot beneath the redbud trees. The grass was brown and poked the soles of her feet, and only a few brown heart-shaped leaves clung to the branches. Still, it was her favorite spot for respite and rest. *Mamm* had loved the redbuds and had *Daed* plant several throughout the yard. Naomi was glad to have something of her parents, especially the wooden bench *Daed* had made for her mother where she could do her stitching.

Naomi stopped short and took several breaths. She waited for the emotion that often came whenever she turned her attention to the bench.

Now, it remained cold and empty. She drew her fingertips over the glossy back, feeling the loss of her mother all over again. None of them had dared to sit in *Mamm*'s spot since her death. A pang filled her chest, and she rubbed at the spot to ease the discomfort. She missed her parents, especially *Mamm*'s sound wisdom. She would know best how to deal with grieving children as well as how Naomi should navigate her marriage with Abe.

Of course, they didn't have a real marriage.

If only Naomi could remember that and quit trying to be a real *fraa*, then her feelings wouldn't be hurt over his absence from the table or anywhere else. Drawing her sleeve over her eyes, she knew she had nobody to blame but herself, but he'd been so good with curbing Caleb's idleness and again with Sara. She shuddered against the emotion working into her eyes. Hadn't his interaction with Daniel produced joyful giggles? And Daniel spoke! She'd rarely heard him utter a noise since he'd been a *boppli*, and yet, he said one word in his attempt to mimic Abe. How could the things Abe accomplished in such a short time not woo her heart?

She chewed the inside of her cheek and glanced toward the house. Earth from fallen leaves decaying into the ground mingled with the sweet scent of cinnamon bread wafting through the windows. With the younger *kinder* resting and the older ones helping Abe, Naomi had thought of working on another quilt for the little consignment shop the *Englischers* liked to visit, but she didn't think she could manage the treadle with her ankle hurting the way it did, and with Rachel at work, she had no one to sew while she trimmed and cut pieces of fabric. So she opted to heed Abe's earlier advice and rest her leg.

Pushing aside memories of her parents, she eased onto the grass, lay down and stared up at the blue sky peeking through the bare branches. In a few months, they would produce the prettiest purple flowers, and then the leaves would come. Soft, cotton-like clouds drifted over her, and she lost herself in the shapes. At least, she tried to, but her thoughts kept racing back to Abe and his absence from the table these last few days. According to Abe's *bruder*, he had a good reason for missing lunch and dinner these past nights, but Naomi couldn't help wondering why fixing the horse's shoe couldn't have waited another hour and why he hadn't shown up for any other meal since. *Daed* wouldn't have missed a grand meal, especially when they typically had cold sandwiches, soups and salads. She'd made Abe's favorite meal, and then she tried several new recipes, even asking Levi what Abe preferred when they lived at home with their parents. She wanted to thank him for all he'd done. She wanted to show him her love.

Where had that thought come from? Sure, she asked *Gotte* to help her love him. She'd said that prayer each morning since their ceremony. She wanted to love him. But *did* she love him? Had that been why she'd been so disappointed he hadn't come to lunch or dinner or any other meal. His absence made her feel as if he was avoiding her. It made her feel…rejected. Again.

A dark shadow grew over her, and she focused her gaze. The object of her thoughts hovered above her. "Mind if I join you?"

She began to rise, but before she could manage the task, Abe lay beside her, his arms folded behind his head and feet crossed at the ankles.

"You'll get your shirt dirty," she said.

A smile teased the corner of his mouth. "I hear my *fraa* has a secret recipe to remove stains."

"You heard that, huh?" she asked.

"Jah," he said. "Straight from her *bruder*'s mouth while we were fixing the clothesline. It shouldn't come down again." Abe pointed through the branches at the clouds. "Is that a rabbit?"

Naomi shook her head. "The nose is too big, and it has wings. Maybe a lion."

"A lion that flies?" He laughed.

"I've heard of stranger things."

"Come to think of it, it does look like it has wings, but the nose is sharpening. Maybe an eagle."

"*Jah*, an eagle," she laughed.

He turned his head and glanced at her. Reaching his hand out, he twined his fingers with hers. The touch, his warmth, shocked her. His calluses locked against hers, but she delighted in the way the two pieces of them fit so nicely together. It was how it had been during their courtship.

"This is good, *jah*?" He seemed comfortable with his actions. Her breathing, on the other hand, hitched and her pulse raced. Was there hope he wanted more than a marriage in name only? Would he stay in Garnett? And without her plans to woo him with her cooking ?

"I wanted to thank you for sending plates out with Levi. It's been nice having my *bruder* around. There's much to do on the farm, and each task is pressing."

"Of course. I understand a thrown shoe is an urgent task." She forced a smile so he didn't see the disappointment his absence had caused.

"It is. We need the horses to remain hale and hearty if they are going to work the fields we won't work with the tractor, and then the plow needed fixing and another gate came loose."

"Never a dull moment around here."

He looked back at the sky. The brim of his hat shielded the upper half of his face, leaving her clueless as to what his eyes might say. "I will miss your cooking when I go back to Haven."

There it was. His intentions remained the same. He would leave as planned, and she was a fool to think a meal would change his mind when he was so set on leaving. She wanted to pull her hand from his, but doing so would let him know she was affected by him, and that wasn't something she could do if she was to keep her heart intact.

"Surely, your cousin's wife cooks."

His laughter rolled over her like honey on a warm biscuit. It was nice, and yet, it wasn't. She had missed this camaraderie between them, and she knew she would miss him deeply when he left. She'd miss the friendship that had come so easily. If only they disliked each other. If only she'd married one of the other men. If only they hadn't required she give up some of her siblings. Then she wouldn't be married to a man she once loved. She grimaced. A man she *did* love. One she thought had loved her, too. She wouldn't become attached to a man who had made it clear he didn't want a wife.

Three months. The time seemed so long, and yet too short. Could it be *Gotte*'s will for Abe to leave, or was it, as she'd told Sara earlier, Abe's own doing? She pushed the longing aside and tried to be content with what Abe offered her, a marriage in name only. Nothing more.

"My cousin isn't married, and his dog doesn't cook," he teased. "We fend for ourselves, which often means peanut butter and jelly sandwiches."

"That sounds *gut*!" she said.

"Not when you eat them every day. Again, *denki* for the meals. They were *wunderbar*."

"It was nothing. A small show of appreciation." She sobered, knowing that was only a partial truth. She'd intentionally made his favorite meal to draw him to the table and into the house more often, not to keep him in the barn. "*Denki*, for all you've done for the *kinder*. Sara's temper has improved over the past few days, and Caleb seems to enjoy the tasks you've given him. And, of course, Daniel."

"I cannot take credit for Daniel. I'm just thankful to be the recipient of his enthusiastic joy. As for Caleb and Sara, I have done nothing more than pay attention to their feelings." He shook his head when she began to turn sullen, as if he sensed her self-recrimination. "Don't, Naomi. You've done *wunderbar* given the circumstances. You are only one person and can't see everything. I'm certain the worries were heavy on your shoulders, and the running of the farm overshadowed your own time to grieve. Knowing you the way I do, you pushed your grief aside while trying to love the *kinder* through theirs. Sometimes it takes someone outside the situation to see what those on the inside can't. Caleb is a man in the making and needs guidance. He craves it, but his age is tender. Part of him wants to be a man, the other part wants to remain a child and have fun. He just needs someone to see his efforts and acknowledge them. He is a *gut* boy. Albeit prone to idleness at times, but a *gut* boy all the same." He sighed. "Sara is another matter, and I believe it is only by *Gotte*'s grace she responded as she did. Although I have a feeling she is up to something. I cannot figure out what that might be just yet."

Naomi cringed. If her sister was up to something, they were all in for trouble. She hoped it was only a prank, like swapping baking powder for baking soda when making cookies for after Sunday service. One boy often teased her, and Sara had planned revenge knowing the double-chocolate walnuts were his favorite. "Well, then, I have a favor to ask. It involves Sara, and I think it will take her mind off any pranks she might be cooking up."

"Of course, what is it?"

Naomi bit her bottom lip. "Will you take the girls shopping for fabrics when you pick up Rachel from work? I wouldn't ask, but I did promise the day all the cows got out. However, my ankle…" She motioned to the object of her irritation.

"I would be honored to take them."

"Are you certain? It can be a challenge, especially when it comes to choosing colors."

"I'm sure they will be fine," he said with that pulse-stealing smile of his.

"Sara can be obstinate about what she wants, but she can also be indecisive about her fabric choices, too."

He continued to smile at her. "Like her older sister, if I recall."

Naomi sucked in a sharp breath. She didn't want to think about their fabric-shopping excursion over two years before. It had taken her hours to choose the right fabric for her wedding dress. She couldn't recall why *Mamm* hadn't been able to go with her or why Abe had taken her instead, but he had, patiently encouraging her, telling her how nice each fabric complemented her complexion or her eyes. That was a memory better left in the past, right along with the heartache. "Oh, look, that cloud looks like a rooster."

"Ah," he said as he released her hand and sat up. "I think it looks like a horse and buggy. Which reminds me, I have a few things to do. I'll take your sisters to town afterward. Will you have them meet me then, at the barn after lunch?"

"*Jah, denki*, Abe."

She'd have to find a way to thank him. Maybe with a mulberry pie, another of his favorites. This time, her intention would be solely to thank him, not to woo him into wanting a true *fraa*.

The rumble of the tractor drowned out most of the girls' constant chatter and giggles, and he felt cheated. He knew some of his friends complained about their noisy sisters, but having spent most of his life in hollow silence, outside of his *daed*'s anger, Abe now liked the incessant noise. Especially when the conversation was filled with so much joy and laughter. It reminded him of happier days and the times he'd spent with Naomi's family. He was glad to know the difficult times and grief hadn't taken their ability to laugh away from them.

He stopped the tractor in front of the café and waited for Rachel. Five minutes later, she walked out the door with a bag and an enthusiastic wave. "This is a nice surprise."

Abe helped Naomi's sister into the truck bed hitched to the back of the tractor, and then waited for her to unfold a lawn chair and sit.

"We're getting new fabric to make dresses," Annie said.

Sara bounced in her lawn chair. "Naomi promised."

"*Jah*, Naomi wanted to come," Abe said. "But she

didn't think she could manage just yet, with her ankle still not healed."

"She probably just wanted us out of the house to clean and bake without us underfoot," Hannah said.

Abe's brow furrowed. "That doesn't make sense. Surely, she'd appreciate the help. And what about Daniel and Zeke?"

Hannah snorted. "Our *schwester* likes things done a certain way."

"*Jah*, but it's fine. She's less anxious when she's cleaning," Rachel said.

The comment left him wondering if that was why Naomi had had a problem with him cooking breakfast for them all.

"*Mamm* was the same way," Rachel added. "As much as I like shopping for fabrics with our *schwester*, I'm glad she stayed home. She's as bad as Sara when it comes to picking out fabrics."

Abe thought back to his conversation with Naomi about Sara and wondered if there was any truth to what Rachel said. He tried to recall the various dresses he'd seen Naomi wear during their courtship, There weren't very many: her black mourning dress, a cornflower-blue one, a dark blue and the light purple dress she'd worn on their wedding day. "I helped her pick out the fabric for her wedding dress."

"Trust me, if you hadn't been with her to offer your opinion, she would have spent hours deciding, only to leave empty-handed." Rachel laughed and then held up a bag. "I brought her favorite treat, sticky buns."

Abe couldn't help but smile. Naomi liked sweets, but she really liked the café's sticky buns. The combination of the sticky, sweet syrup dripping over the side with the pecans on top made Naomi's eyes close each time she sank her teeth into a roll. He'd taken her on several dates to the café just so he could watch pleasure light Naomi's face while she ate the treat. What else did she like? What could he get for her that would make her smile and let her know he appreciated the meals she'd cooked for him? "She'll like that very much, *jah*?"

He wished he'd thought of it before Rachel had. Now, he couldn't think of anything else she might like. His mind was like a dark room with no light. Not a single idea of what to get her formed in his head.

"She works so hard, I thought she needed something to enjoy."

"That is very kind and thoughtful of you, Rachel," Abe said.

"I brought enough for everyone, too." She grinned.

"Denki," he said. "Let's get to the store before it's too late."

He climbed back onto the tractor and turned the key. The motor roared to life, and the engine started vibrating.

In a few minutes, he halted the tractor in front of the fabric store and jumped down. He scanned the road for approaching vehicles and noticed the square was crowded with vehicles parked around it. He strode toward the pickup bed behind the tractor.

Sara was climbing over the tailgate when Abe stopped her. "I know you're excited, but are you supposed to fold your chair or leave it?"

With an exaggerated roll of her eyes, Sara stormed to the lawn chair, folded it and laid it on the two-by-fours that formed the bed of the trailer. Hannah helped Annie from her lawn chair, folded their chairs and then climbed over the edge of the trailer. Abe swung Annie over the side and set her feet on the ground. He was glad to see her wearing shoes for a change.

"Are you coming?" Sara asked as she climbed over the side.

"Jah," he said. "After I come back from the grocery store. You know Naomi's expectations, *jah*?"

"We do," Rachel said. "I'll make sure we choose *gut*."

"Denki," Abe said, then he drove the tractor a few blocks to the country store and parked on the far side of the parking lot. Since this was the first time he'd been in town since his return to Garnett, he'd taken note of some of the changes as he drove past. A few businesses had closed in the two years since he'd been gone, but there were new ones, too, and he was glad of it. He was glad to see the small grocery store was still there and hoped they hadn't changed the inventory around too much. He liked knowing where things were.

He climbed down, hunched into his coat against the brisk wind and walked across the gravel drive. There was one other tractor, a few buggies and a few cars. The various vehicles were commonplace in towns with Amish communities. Most of the cars were *Englischers* wanting to experience the Amish ways. He didn't mind speaking with the locals, but he wasn't sure how he felt about being a spectacle. He'd experienced that more often than he liked in Haven working at the grocery store. Always being stared at and spoken to like he was a foreigner who didn't understand the English language.

The sun slid behind a cloud, leaving him cloaked in its

shadow. He looked to the sky and smiled to himself. The cloud was in the shape of a dog, and the one in front of it looked like a duck. He had enjoyed lying in the grass beside Naomi while they looked at clouds. He had enjoyed holding her hand even more and wanted to do it again. The peace he'd experienced at her side had always settled in his bones and soothed him and made him believe the trials and tribulations on this earth could be overcome with the small things. Like holding hands with his *fraa*.

He didn't think anything had ever felt so right before. The softness of her palm against his callouses had been more than he'd expected or hoped for. The way their fingers married together had solidified a Scripture in Genesis he'd always wondered about. It was not good for man to be alone, which was why *Gotte* created Eve. If that was true, why was Abe sentenced to such a life?

He pulled open the door to the country store and nodded to the two men in straw hats sitting at the white folding table sipping coffee. A young couple sat at the other end of the table, sharing a thick cinnamon roll. Abe's stomach grumbled, and if Rachel hadn't already gotten a sweet treat, he would have ordered several cinnamon rolls.

Deciding against taking up a basket, he strolled toward the bread and grabbed two loaves. He started to head toward the peanut butter and jelly, when a conversation filtering over the shelves stopped him dead in his tracks.

"It's hard not to feel sorry for her," the first female voice said.

"Oh, *jah*! He left her once before, and she nearly be-

came a recluse. Remember, we couldn't get her to come
to the quilting gatherings?"

"I heard he'd only offered to marry her the first time
because he felt sorry for her, but then he left."

"*Jah*, Ira says he'll leave again once he realizes Naomi
and the *kinder* are too much work."

Ira? Ira Beachy? Abe seethed when he realized who
was gossiping about him and Naomi. Grace Beachy,
Naomi's childhood friend. She had even stood beside
her during the ceremony with her husband, Ira. They
supported her in her decision to take Abe as a husband.
What kind of friends were they?

"He said *nae* man wants a hobbling *fraa*."

"*Jah*, what a waste. I would have married Abe in a
heartbeat. He should have married for love and not pity.
He deserves better than what she can give."

The loaf of bread suffered beneath his clenched fist.
He was half tempted to leave the store without his purchases and started to do so, but his gut stopped him.
Had Naomi endured this kind of ridicule and malicious
gossip when he'd left the first time? Did they say she'd
become a recluse after he'd left? Would Naomi endure
more when he left again? He stalked around the corner
of the aisle and waited for the women to acknowledge
him. He tried to place the other girl, and knew he'd
gone to church with her, but the more he tried to recall
her name, the more anger surged in his veins. He was
tempted to stay in Garnett just to get these women and
those who gossiped liked them to quiet their busybodies.

Grace, the shorter and prettier of the two, pulled a
jar of relish from the shelf and then looked up at him.

"Oh, Abe. *Gut daag*," she said with a sweet smile as if she hadn't been gossiping about his wife.

"Gut daag," he said.

The other one looked at him with wide, round eyes.

"I understand you have questions about my intentions toward Naomi." When they didn't speak, he continued. "Not that it is any of your business, but I did not marry Naomi out of pity. And furthermore, you two would do well to emulate her. She is the kindest and most courageous woman I know. And she obviously has a stern enough backbone to face malicious gossip being spread, especially by someone she believes is her friend."

Grace looked shocked at the accusation.

"Do you deny it?" he asked.

"We are sorry, Abe," the taller, brown-haired, mousy one, whose name he couldn't recall, said. "We misunderstood what we heard."

"Maybe you shouldn't speak about things you've heard at all when you don't know the full story." Heat flared against his nostrils. "Especially about people. You might hurt their feelings."

They stared at him, both a little red-faced and contrite. He softened his tone. "I'll have you know, I care for Naomi very much, and I—" He almost said he loved her, but he stopped himself before he said anything more. He didn't want anyone to know the truth stirring in his heart, how Naomi made him feel alive and *gut* whenever he was with her. "I cannot believe the two of you have stooped to speak badly about Naomi. Your friend Grace." He shook his head. "I hope you will consider your words more carefully before you speak. I wouldn't want my wife to hear your ill manners."

And with that, he grabbed a jar of peanut butter and a jar of homemade grape jam. He placed his items on the counter and noticed a display filled with vegetable and flower seeds. It was way too early to plant and he was surprised to find them on the shelf before the New Year. The seeds weren't the wave petunias she favored in the spring, but the images on the packages were bright and colorful. He wasn't certain she'd like them, but if they brought her some joy, they'd be worth the purchase. He picked several varieties, each reminding him of Naomi's sunshiny smile. He walked out of the grocery store with his purchases feeling much lighter than he had only moments before. The thought of giving Naomi the flowers, even if they were only seeds, cooled his ire some, and by the time he arrived back at the fabric store, his anger had calmed completely. At least toward the women, not with himself. His leaving Garnett had caused Naomi more heartache than he knew.

How could he ever do that to her again?

Chapter Nine

Naomi punched the risen dough and split it into four. She rolled each one into a ball and coated them with flour, then rolled them out into flat disk shapes. She enjoyed the quiet of the house while the boys played with their toys, but missed her *schwesters* and worried over their fabric selections. She hoped they didn't convince Abe into buying anything inappropriate.

When she'd been young, she'd wished to wear something bold and beautiful. Something bright pink or bold blue or even something with a small pattern on it, but it wasn't the Amish way. Thinking about it now, she was glad *Mamm* had guided her to the appropriate fabrics. She nearly laughed imagining the small flower prints that might have made her look like a walking wall of flowers. She shuddered. She'd seen a magazine article once at the store where such prints were used to paper the *Englischer*'s walls.

Abe had gone shopping with her once before, so he knew what to expect with her sisters. At the rumble of the tractor, Naomi jumped from the chair and hobbled toward the kitchen window. She allowed herself to smile at the joy emanating from her sisters' faces, but her smile quickly fell when she noticed the hard set of Abe's chin. Even though his straw hat shielded most of his face, she could tell he was not happy, and wondered what had happened. Whatever it was, her sisters seemed completely unfazed.

Naomi went out onto the porch and waved. Caleb and Levi appeared from the barn. The tractor came to a stop in front of the house, and Naomi smiled as her *schwesters* exited the wagon. Their grins and laughter were so rare these last months that they did Naomi good.

"How did it go?" she asked. Her question was directed at Abe, but it was Sara who answered.

"Gut, jah?" Sara turned to Hannah, Rachel and Annie for confirmation.

"Jah, it was very good," Rachel said. "We wish you could have come too." Her sister climbed the stairs and looked pointedly at Naomi's injured foot. "How are you doing? I hope you've found some time to rest."

She sensed Abe's eyes on her and looked his way. "I am *gut*. It will get better, and soon we'll be able to shop together. Now, show me what you bought."

"Me first." Annie sank her hand into her bag and pulled out a pretty pink that reminded Naomi of a fading sunset. It was *wunderbar* for a seven-year-old. The youngest of her sisters handed her the fabric, and Naomi rubbed the softness between her thumb and forefinger. "Very nice, Annie. Did you pick it out yourself?"

She nodded with a huge grin.

"I did, too," Sara said as she pulled out a beautiful lavender.

"Oh, that's pretty."

"Hannah didn't." Annie's bottom lip turned into a pout. "Abe had to help her choose."

"Really?" Naomi asked. "And what did Abe choose for you, *liebling*?"

Hannah frowned. By this time, Abe had climbed down from the tractor and stood near the porch stairs. Hannah glanced at him over her shoulder and then produced her fabric. It was the shade of dirt. Naomi gasped. She looked over at Abe.

He shrugged. "Of all her color choices, I thought this one best suited her."

Rachel laughed. "You're not telling the full truth. Hannah wanted a green the color of lime Jell-O. Her next choice wasn't any better. Abe entered the store in the middle of our, uh…discussion."

Naomi didn't need to hear anymore to know Abe had walked in on an argument. She was just thankful Sara hadn't been at the center and had a meltdown in town.

"It wasn't as bad as that," Abe said, scratching his patchy jaw. As was their custom, Amish men didn't shave once they were married, and Abe's beard was growing in nicely. A little darker than his brown hair, it would be thick in no time, and he'd be even more handsome than he already was. "Although the clerk may have thought differently."

Sara snorted. "Mary knows us well. She owns the store."

"That she does," Naomi laughed. The sound was even more foreign to her than her siblings' laughter. "I can't believe she didn't step…" Naomi trailed her words off, not wanting to hurt Hannah's or Abe's feelings, but the color was drab and lifeless.

"Step in and make a better choice?" Abe lifted his straw hat from his head. Naomi wanted to sink her fingers into his curls to see if they were as soft as they looked.

"No, that's not what I meant. Hannah just tends toward blues and greens."

"Well," Sara said, "she did try to pick a green."

"And a blue," Abe said. "But it had a small pattern on it and I didn't think you would approve. We did find some buttons, though."

"Buttons?" Naomi asked.

Abe's cheeks burned bright red. Her heart skittered, and then raced after she caught her breath. He was handsome. Probably the most handsome man she'd ever met. Oh, what it would be like to be a real married couple where they could steal kisses or hold hands whenever they wished. Her face grew warm remembering their earlier moment. It'd been sweet and tender. It'd been just as she'd imagined since the first time Abe asked to court her. But it'd only been a moment, nothing more, and soon they would live their separate lives. She would live in Garnett, and he in Haven. She shook off her thoughts before it stole the joy away.

"Yes, buttons."

The young girls in their community used pins on their clothes until they reached womanhood, and then they were allowed to wear buttons. Was this the reason for Abe's scowl as he pulled into the yard?

"Oh!" she said, reaching out her hand. "Let me see."

Hannah handed her a pack of plain round buttons and said, "I hoped we could cover them with fabric."

"Oh, of course. I'll show you how." She figured it was

time to release Abe from the uncomfortable situation. "*Denki*, and I'm sorry I couldn't go."

"You're welcome. I suppose I should get back to chores before dinner."

Her heart soared. Did that mean he would join them? She hoped so as she made another casserole with sausage, cabbage, carrots, onions and apples. The scents had permeated the kitchen, leaving her both hungry and hopeful that Abe would finally join them at the table tonight.

"Oh, and don't forget," Rachel said, holding up a bag from the diner where she worked. "I have sticky buns for a treat afterward."

"What a nice surprise." Naomi clapped her hands together. "It will be nice to have a full table again with Abe and Levi coming together."

Instantly, she swallowed back the grief that washed over her. Two chairs at their table had remained empty for over ten months. A stark reminder of her parents' absence. Abe took his place there the morning he'd made breakfast, but he hadn't been back since. Only his *bruder*, Levi. She'd been trudging along trying to be both *mamm* and *daed* while also working the farm. It was time to let others help her care for her siblings and her home. She knew she couldn't do it alone any longer.

She felt his hand on hers and looked into eyes full of compassion. "It will be our honor to fill your table for the evening meal, Naomi," Abe said.

Abe hefted the axe against the trunk of a rotted tree. He swung it once, twice, and then with all the frustration bottled up from the day, he swung it a third time. The tree remained standing. He felt like collapsing.

"Abe?" Naomi's sweet voice trickled over him, and he immediately felt his irritation give way. "I've brought some lemonade. You look like you could use it?"

He couldn't help the smile. *"Denki."*

"I wanted to thank you again for taking the girls fabric shopping," she said, looking across the field. "I hope it wasn't too awful."

The lemony sweet liquid danced along his taste buds as he took a sip from the cup. He savored the sensation as he considered his response. How could he talk to her about the gossip without hurting her? His best course of action was to be direct and straight to the point.

"Naomi, will you sit with me awhile?" He motioned to a spot beneath another tree. One he hadn't begun hacking away at.

At her nod, they walked over and sat beneath the tree. Once they were seated and his lemonade glass empty, he asked, "What was it like after I left?"

She looked surprised by his question. "I don't understand."

He spun the glass in his hand, staring through the clear bottom to the blades of grass. "I heard gossip about you. Us. And it wasn't kind."

She plucked a piece of grass from the ground and began knotting it. "Gossip rarely is kind, Abe."

"I'm sorry."

She shook her head. "You don't need to apologize for other people's misdoings."

He gave in to the need to hold her hand and twined his fingers with hers. "You constantly amaze and surprise me. Your grace and forgiveness toward others is admirable."

She laughed. "Don't think my light shines so bright, Abe. I have a long way to go in forgiving. The gossip is the reason I avoid town when I can."

"Because of me?"

"No, not because of you," she said. "Yes, I blamed you for a long time, but they are responsible for their own wrongdoings, you for yours. Your rejection hurt me."

His rejection? Is that what she thought, that he rejected her?

"Their speculation as to why you rejected me hurt even more."

He squeezed her hand. "Naomi, I didn't reject you."

Pulling her hand from his, she hugged her legs to her chest. "It's okay, Abe. I understand now that you didn't want a *fraa*. Maybe you married me now for the wrong reasons, and I agreed for the right ones. People will decide their own truth, but our truth is you didn't want a wife and now you have one."

"I—" He stopped himself for a moment, then went on. "I did leave, but not for the reasons you think."

His heart beat hard against his chest wall. He wanted to tell her the truth, but he couldn't.

He turned toward her and lifted her chin so she would look him in the eye. "You're right, I didn't want a wife, but if I did, it would have been you. There is no better *fraa* than you, Naomi."

Shaking her head, she said, "Please, Abe. You can't be serious. You've had to carry half my chores and take time away from yours to tend to the *kinder*."

"I am serious, Naomi." The moment he spoke, he knew it to be true. There was no better woman than Naomi Lambright—no, Dienner. He only wished he could be worthy of her somehow. "I am sorry for my part in the malicious gossip, and I'm afraid I might have fanned the fires even more."

Then he told her about his encounter with Grace Beachy and her friend at the country store.

A trickle of laughter spilled from her. "I would have liked to have seen their faces." She sobered. "*Denki* for defending me."

"Of course, it's what *manns* do for their *fraas*." He wanted to do more for her, like take long walks with her and even longer buggy rides. He wanted to sit beside her on the sofa in front of the fireplace while they both read books. He wanted to watch clouds with her. He wanted to take her in his arms. He wanted to kiss her. He wanted to…love her. "Oh, here, I have something for you."

He jumped to his feet and helped her to hers. He looped his arm through hers to keep her steady as he walked at her pace to the barn. He guided her inside. A cow mooed; one of the horses neighed. Four chickens strutted around pecking at the floor, and a baby goat bleated. He drew the life of the barn into his lungs. The scent of hay and livestock were part of his blood.

She gasped. "Oh, Abe! This is *wunderbar*. The barn looks *gut*, *jah*?"

"*Denki*," he said, "but this isn't your surprise."

He strode over to the workbench and plucked a white paper bag off the counter. "Here, I thought you might like these."

She took the bag from him and he watched as she peeked inside. She gasped. "Oh, Abe, this is the prettiest shade of blue I've ever seen. It's the color of the sky just before the sun sets in the west." She held it up to a ray of light pouring through the open barn door. "It's almost purple."

"You like it, *jah*?" he asked with expectancy.

"*Jah*, it's *wunderbar*," she said, her words a mere whisper.

"I picked it out," he said. "It complements your eyes."

She pulled more of the fabric from the bag and he heard something fall. Glancing down, he saw several packets of the seeds on the dirt floor. He bent down and handed them to her.

"I noticed the flower bed was overflowing with weeds, and I sent Caleb and Hannah to clean it out. But I thought we could plant them together when spring comes. I remember how much you like flowers."

Her eyes sparkled, and he knew in that moment that he wanted, needed, to see that light shine more often. Every day wouldn't be enough for him.

For the first time since his return, the worry lines that had marred her brow and the corners of her mouth dissipated. Her complexion glowed, and she looked more beautiful than he'd ever seen her. He realized that he wanted to kiss her. Not a brief touch of their lips as they had done on their wedding, but a real kiss.

"*Denki*, I would love that, Abe."

There was that word again. *Love.* He wasn't sure how to connect what he knew with what others seemed to know. He recalled the Bible saying love was patient, love was kind and did not keep a record of wrongs, but that wasn't the love he'd learned from his *daed* in their family. That was the love Naomi showed to her *brudres* and *schwesters*. It was the love she had shown him and the love he wanted her to show him now. It was what he wanted to give her. Were the feelings he experienced whenever he was with Naomi or thought about her love? His insides quaked at the thought. Not in fear but in excitement.

Could he keep himself from being the kind of man his *daed* was? Scenes of violence played in his head. *Mamm*'s bruises, Levi's broken arm, his own bloodied lip. He wanted the *gut* love, not the bad. "Or maybe you'd rather plant them with the *kinder.*"

Then the worry lines returned, and he wanted to kick himself. He was all twisted up inside, wanting to see her happy and smiling one moment and regretting it the next. Seeing her smile only made him want to see more. It drew him to her like bees to honey. If he continued on this path of courting his *fraa*, she'd only get hurt, just like *Mamm*. He would never do that to Naomi, but the only way he saw to keep that from happening was to keep his distance. To stay as far from her as possible.

"I would like that, too, I suppose," she said, and he couldn't help noticing her choice of words. "I'm sure they will as well. It's something we did with our *mamm* every year."

"I remember," he said, recalling how bright and colorful the landscape around the Lambright farmhouse always looked. He wondered if his own *mamm* liked flowers. She'd never planted them and had never brought any into the house as far as he knew.

"But, I'd like even better if we all did it as a family, *jah*? You, me and the *kinder.*"

He nodded and swallowed down the knot of emotion forming in his throat.

"Well, I should get back to chopping a few trees.

They're rotten, and we wouldn't want a strong wind to blow them over and cause problems."

"*Denki*, for the seeds. The yard will seem much brighter once we get all of them planted in the spring."

"It will," he said. Her eyes remained bright and sparkly like stars in the sky, even in the dimness of the barn. He reached out and brushed his finger down the side of her jaw. "You're beautiful, Naomi. Inside and out."

He heard the slight hitch in her breath. He drew her into his arms. As he held her close, she leaned into him. The sweet scent of her lavender soap dizzied him. He whispered in her ear, "You're a *wunderbar* woman, Naomi. A *wunderbar fraa*."

He delighted that she didn't pull away or argue with him. She just accepted his compliments, as she should. Of their own accord, his lips kissed hers. Once, twice, three times. It was the sweetest sensation he'd ever known. His mind reeled. He shouldn't be doing this, kissing her. Loving her. But he'd spent two years away from her and the past few weeks watching her in annoyed silence. Every turn he made, he saw her strength and courage as she tried to keep her family together and keep the farm going the best she could. Where others saw her weakness and her disability, he saw the most amazing woman he'd ever encountered. She was his *fraa*. His companion and helpmate. His wife. She owned his heart, and when he left, he'd be leaving it here with her and the *kinder*. Drawing in a breath, he prepared to release her.

"I am sorry for causing you pain. I wish I could turn back time, Naomi." He never would have left. He would have stayed by her side, facing the gossips together. "I'm sorry you endured such malicious talk. They don't know you like I do."

Closing his eyes against the wetness on his cheeks, he relished the ache in his heart at what could never be. Yes, she was his *fraa*, but they could never have a real marriage. He never should have allowed himself to hope for something better for himself. He never should have allowed himself to hope, but he had. He still did, but couldn't continue to, and that cut him deeply.

"Abe," she whispered. "I forgive you."

He pulled away and turned his back to her. "I don't deserve your forgiveness."

The tenderness of her hand touched his shoulder. "That isn't for you to decide, Abe"

Then she left him standing alone in the barn. He couldn't bring himself to turn around and watch her walk away. If he did, he might call her back.

An hour later, Abe sat at the kitchen table with Naomi, her siblings and his *bruder*, Levi. Excited chatter filled the room, but Abe couldn't find it in himself to join the conversation. His mind kept thinking about their kisses. His heart tossed a line and hooked onto the forgiveness she'd given, but he kept telling himself she didn't really know the truth of who he was. His *daed*'s blood and anger ran thick in his veins.

The room filled with laughter, and he noticed Naomi holding her palm to her chest as she threw her head back and laughed. What had he missed? He glanced around the table until his attention fell on Levi.

"You remember th-th-that, Abe?" Levi asked.

Abe shrugged. "I'm sorry, I wasn't paying attention."

"It's obvious you're not paying any attention at all," Naomi said, motioning to the empty fork Abe was about to slip into his mouth. How long had he been like that, holding his fork with nothing on it?

"I was thinking," he said as he looked directly at Naomi. She blushed.

"No work at the table," she said. "That was *Mamm*'s rule. She said there's plenty of time to do work once your belly is full."

Abe tilted his head to the side and thought about that for a moment. All they'd ever talked about at his childhood home was chores needing to be done and chores that didn't get done right. There had never been any other conversation.

"I think it's a *g-g-gut* rule," Levi said. "Now, do you remember the old hound we had who liked chasing baby skunks?"

He remembered. "*Jah*, and their *mamm* wasn't too happy about it."

"Neither was ours, when Orlie chased them into the barn. All three of us were banned from the house."

"Oh, I imagine you stunk awful," Naomi laughed.

"Ewwww," Zeke squealed as he pinched his nose. Daniel mimicked his little *bruder*.

"I'd like sleeping in the barn," Caleb said.

"Not in ours—you'd smell up the horses," Hannah said.

"I suppose you're right." Levi wiped his mouth with a napkin. "We were there an entire week."

Abe laughed. "*Jah*, we slept in the barn but had to stay away from the horses. *Daed* didn't want them stinking when he pulled them out to work." It had been the best week of his entire childhood. He didn't fear being woken up by his father for something that hadn't gotten done right.

"Remember, *Mamm* snuck peanut butter and jelly sandwiches and peach cobbler to us."

The memory drew Abe back to that time; he'd been twelve, Caleb's age, and Levi eight. He'd forgotten about the sandwiches, but he hadn't forgotten the boisterous hollering he'd heard each night as he and Levi climbed into the loft to sleep. "I noticed a piece of loose sheeting on the barn roof when I saw *Mamm* the other day." Abe drew in a breath. His brother had been staying in the barn with him for the past several days, and not once had they spoke of home. Abe hadn't the courage to bring up the past when his brother seemed so happy, but now, he had to know what'd been happening there. "I'm surprised *Daed* hasn't had it fixed. Why is that?"

Levi laid his fork on his plate and leaned against the back of his chair. He met Abe's eyes and then shook his head. "I don't know. I haven't been home in two years. I left a few days after you. Thanks to Naomi's *daed*."

Chapter Ten

Naomi sat on the ground beside one of the flower beds and pulled the last of the dead flowers the *kinder* had missed. Spring was several months away, but with the weather fair, it was nice to soak up the sun and busy her hands with work she enjoyed. Zeke and Daniel scooped dirt with the spoons she'd given them. The girls had made themselves scarce. And Abe, Caleb and Levi were out in the field somewhere. She didn't mind pulling the weeds and old flowers since she enjoyed getting her hands into the sun-kissed dirt, but it would have been nice to have company, especially Abe.

It had been a few days since he'd brought the flower seeds home and suggested they plant them together when the time came, but his odd silence over the past few days and renewed absence from the dinner table had her worried.

Would he leave sooner than three months? She didn't want to bother him with yet another chore and possibly push him out of Garnett. Besides, she was determined to get the ground ready for the spring planting. She'd already planned out where she would place the various seeds, and hoped the flower bed would look as good as she imagined when they were in full bloom.

It also gave her something to do besides think about the conversation between Levi and Abe at the dinner table the other night. Except, that was all she was doing. How had Abe not known his own *bruder* had left home too? And what had her *daed* done to cause Levi to leave?

Those questions had plagued her the last few nights as she tried to sleep. And no matter how much her curiosity ate at her, she couldn't bring herself to ask Abe. The topic had obviously shocked and bothered him, because as soon as Levi mentioned her *daed*, Abe cut the conversation off by motioning for Levi to follow him outside.

She speared the tip of the weeder into the dirt and wedged it beneath the root of one weed. It broke free, and she tossed it into her pail.

The other part of the conversation niggling at her was the story about the skunk and sleeping in the barn. Why did Abe's *mamm* sneak food out to the boys when they were little? Were they not allowed to eat in the barn?

Using the little spade, she dug a hole deep and wide enough to pull out a stubborn root. She pulled her plans for the flower bed from a book she had by her side and compared it to the actual flower bed. Would there be enough room to add wave petunias, too? She liked the way they took over and filled the empty spots, sometimes overflowing into the yard. She looked at her plans and how the colors were in perfect symmetry on paper, but the past year had been chaos. Chaos she'd fought hard to keep in order and failed, until Abe rescued her and the *kinder*. She wasn't so sure she wanted a plan for the spring flowers. What if they embraced the chaos and planted the flowers without any rhyme or reason? What if she let Zeke and Daniel place the flowers where they wanted?

"What do you think, boys?" she asked, standing. "Would you like to help plant the flowers when the time comes?"

"Gut, gut, gut," Zeke said, dancing around in circles.

"G-g-gut," Daniel said with a huge grin.

"Yes, *gut*, Daniel!" She hugged him to her side. She wiped her hands on her apron and admired her work with a smile. "Soon, spring will be here, and the flower bed will overflow with lots of color." She placed her flower bed plans back into her book. "Now, how about we go visiting?"

She had a pie cooling on the counter and two loaves of bread she intended to take to Abe's *mamm*. It was time she visited her mother-in-law, and her ankle was finally healed enough that she thought she could drive the buggy herself. Hitching it to the harness might be a problem, but she'd figure it out. She'd done it before, with Rachel's help and without a sore ankle, but she could push through any discomfort. Abe might not be happy about it, but since he'd been avoiding her, eating peanut butter and jelly sandwiches for his meals, he probably wouldn't even know she'd left the house.

After she washed up then cleaned Daniel and Zeke, she harnessed Fern and moved the buggy into place so the arms of the buggy would slide smoothly into the leather straps. She patted Fern's rump, took a moment to catch her breath before she loaded the boys into the buggy along with the treats and headed toward the Dienners' farm. Before she made it too far down the drive, she tested her foot against the brake. Although her ankle hurt a little, it didn't send a sharp, nagging pain up her leg.

Once she was on the road, she relaxed and nearly giggled when she didn't get stopped by Abe or one of the *kinder*. She lifted her chin and allowed the fall breeze to bathe her cheeks. The air was humid in a way she'd expect in spring, not fall. And even though the clouds to the west looked like they held rain, she wouldn't complain. The fields needed all the moisture they could get.

A rabbit ran out into the road. Naomi pulled the reins and stomped on the pedal brake. Pain tore through her ankle and up her leg. She jerked her foot off the brake and allowed Fern to have her lead. She was nervous about driving with her ankle still sore, but the freedom to do something for herself thrilled her and gave her a sense of accomplishment. However, she breathed a sigh of relief the moment the Dienners' drive came into view.

She tightened the reins and shifted to use her other foot to set the brake and then noticed Abe's *mamm* frowning from the steps.

"Hallo," Naomi said, waving as she pulled Zeke and then Daniel out of the buggy. *"Gut* afternoon."

Martha Dienner didn't say a word, and Naomi suddenly doubted the wisdom of bringing gifts to her mother-in-law, but since she was here, she might as well drop off the gifts.

"I've brought you some fresh baked bread and a pie," Naomi said as she lifted the basket from the bench seat. "Come along, boys."

Abe's *mamm* descended the porch steps, her mouth set in a tight line. She looked to Zeke, Daniel and then to Naomi. "They remind me of my boys."

Naomi smiled. "*Jah*, they are *gut* boys." She opened the basket and brought out a loaf of bread.

"You shouldn't be here." Martha glanced toward the barn.

A knot formed in Naomi's stomach. She'd wondered why Abe's *mamm* hadn't come to their wedding, and now she knew. She didn't like her. Wasn't she good enough for Abe? Naomi swallowed down the doubt since their marriage wasn't real, but still, would Abe's *mamm* ever accept her as his wife? To hopefully ease her concerns, Naomi said, "Our marriage is real only in the eyes of *Gotte* and the church. He will leave as soon as the bishop is satisfied."

Martha kept silent, and Naomi set the bread and pie onto the rail of the porch. "Daniel, can you get the flower seed packets, please?"

"Naomi, please, *nae*."

The plea in Martha's voice gave Naomi pause, but she wanted to do something for Abe before he left Garnett, and that meant trying to reconcile Abe with his *mamm*.

"Your *sohn* is a *gut* man. He is honorable and meant no disrespect to you and Henry by marrying me."

Daniel came back with the flower seeds and held them up to Martha. Sadness filled her eyes, even as she smiled at Daniel.

"What is going on here?" Henry Dienner's thundering boom unnerved her, but it was the rifle resting against his shoulder that scared her more. Most Amish farmers had rifles, but she'd only seen *Daed* hold a rifle on a few occasions, to teach them how to use it if a coyote threatened one of their livestock.

"*Gut daag*, Henry," Naomi said. She'd seen Abe's fa-

ther a few times in town with his wife, and even fewer
times at church services over the years, but she'd never
spoken to him, not even at their wedding ceremony or
back when she and Abe had courted. He never smiled and
didn't seem overly friendly, mostly keeping to himself
and leaving before the meals were served after Sunday
service. "We made some bread and a pie. And brought
some flower seeds."

"Denki," he said. "Martha, take the goods in. I'll be
along in a moment."

Naomi flinched at the demand in his voice and the
way Abe's *mamm* jumped. She'd never heard her father
speak to her mother that way, and though Abe's high-
handedness irritated her, he'd only acted that way when
it came to her health and her refusal to let her leg mend.
She owed Abe an apology for being so stubborn.

Abe's *daed* looked pointedly at the boys. "These your
brudres?"

"*Jah*, my youngest *brudres*."

"You expect *my* son to raise them to be *gut* Amish
men?"

"He is *gut* with them," she said, not knowing how else
to respond.

"You should have married Jacob Haver and sent the
kinder to live elsewhere. You've *no* business raising children and *no* business marrying my *sohn*. He'll never
bring you into submission as a *fraa* should be."

Naomi gasped. How dare he say such a thing? She'd
heard Bishop Mueller say she should marry and send the
kinder away, but never with such vehemence or anger.
She'd never heard any man speak so freely about bringing a wife into "submission." What did that even mean?

It sounded too much like bringing a hound to heel, as if she were to be completely obedient to her master.

She felt the sting of Henry's words settle in her stomach. She wanted to cry. No one had ever spoken to her with such hate. And it wasn't because she hobbled around like a injured horse, but because she was a *fraa* in need of submission. He narrowed his eyes and glared at the boys. She pushed Daniel and Zeke behind her as if she could protect them from Henry's anger.

"They are my *brudres* and *schwesters*. I love them and can care for them unlike anyone else."

"Love has nothing to do with raising *kinder* or keeping wives. You're a woman," he said. "You lack the ability to discipline *kinder*. Before you know it, they'll be of an age to cause problems for the community. We have enough shenanigans around here as it is."

This was the man who raised Abe and Levi? No wonder they'd both left home. How had Abe become the man he was now under such harsh parenting? Children needed love and compassion in addition to discipline. They needed guidance and shared wisdom. From what she could surmise from Abe's *daed*, love hadn't been a part of Abe's upbringing.

"I'm sorry to have bothered you," she said, wanting to leave as fast as she could.

"Don't bother us again, Naomi Lambright."

She wanted to correct him and say "Naomi Dienner," but she stayed silent, worried that any show of defiance might irritate him more.

"And tell my *sohn* he better keep his word."

Naomi wondered what he meant by that. The man

scowled, his dark gaze as gray and stormy as the clouds rolling in. When had the sun disappeared?

"And what word is that, Henry?" she asked, trembling.

"That he'll leave town and never come back."

Naomi sucked in a sharp breath. *Was this man the reason Abe couldn't stay? Why he had to leave? But why?* If she could find out, maybe she could fix things and then he could stay.

He took a threatening step closer just as thunder cracked overhead. His nostrils flared. "You see, he isn't the man you think he is." Abe's *daed* drew his long, wrinkled index finger down the side of his forehead. "See this?"

Naomi nodded.

"He did this to me," he said. "And if you're not careful, he'll do the same to you."

She tried to comprehend what Abe's *daed* was saying. But she knew one thing for certain: Abe didn't have a mean bone in his body.

"He'll leave, if he knows what's good for him. And you," he added, emphasizing his words with a bruising jab of his finger to her shoulder, "you don't want the *kinder* getting hurt, do you?"

Naomi drew in a shuddering breath and stepped away from him just as large raindrops fell on her head. She wasn't sure what he'd meant by the threat. Did he think Abe would hurt her siblings? No, Abe wouldn't hurt anyone. He didn't have it in him, but she feared his *fater* might.

"For sure and for certain, Abe will keep his word if it was made without duress or threats." She should have stopped there, but she felt the need to defend her *mann* and deny the accusation his *daed* laid at her feet. Abe couldn't have raised a hand to his *daed*, could he? "Abe Dienner is the most honorable man I know, and he keeps his word."

She didn't know why Abe had left town or what had happened, but she knew he wouldn't have hurt his *daed* like he claimed. And he'd never hurt her or the *kinder*, not intentionally.

Henry's laughter barked at her like a rabid dog. "If that is what you believe, you are more of a fool than I expected."

Lightning zipped across the sky, chased by a boom of thunder, and Naomi rushed the boys to the buggy. She released the brake and nudged Fern with the reins. The rain came down hard, slicing into the buggy from the driver's side, and the wind tore at their clothes. She pulled a blanket from the compartment in the back and handed it to Daniel.

"Here, boys," she said. "Get on the floor and cover up."

She wanted to give Fern the lead, but with each burst of thunder, the horse pulled and yanked, threatening to bolt. It took all of Naomi's strength to keep her steady. "Whoa, girl. It's okay. Slow and steady wins the race, *jah*?"

Lightning split the sky with the crack of thunder. Fern reared her front legs, and Naomi screamed.

Abe wiped the rain from his face as he guided the tractor through the field toward the barn. Caleb and Levi sat on the back bench and huddled into their shirts. The storm had come unexpectedly, and he thanked *Gotte* Naomi was at home with the *kinder*. Rachel was at work at the diner and would be fine, but he hoped the others had gone to the house at the first hint of the storm.

He'd avoided Naomi the last few days, and he wasn't sure why, but he thought it might have to do with what Levi had told him the other night about how Naomi's *daed* had showed up looking for Abe. Soon after Jeremiah Lambright's arrival, he had Bishop Mueller and the deacons come to the house. Levi didn't know what had been said, but their *daed* had allowed Levi to leave with Jeremiah. He'd taken Levi to live with Trevor Meinhardt, a Mennonite who lived ten miles outside town and wasn't just Levi's driver, but his boss, too.

Knowing Levi had escaped their *daed*'s violence had released something in Abe, but it was more than that. If the elders knew of their *fater*'s abuse, were they free of him? Free of the dark secret that had plagued them all through their childhood? Was *Mamm*? Could Abe stay in Garnett with Naomi? Would she let him, or would she hold him to his word and ask him to leave? Those were the questions that kept him awake at night and gnawed at him throughout the day. He wasn't sure how she felt, and that bothered him, and yet he didn't have the courage to ask her or to tell her how he felt about her.

She had said that she forgave him for the past, but did that mean she could love him?

"Once we get the tractor in the barn, let's bring the cows in, too," he hollered over the roaring wind and rain. He didn't want them to be hit with hail or lightning.

He slowed the tractor down and pulled into the barn. Before he'd even shut the tractor off, Hannah, Sara and Annie were shouting at him.

"Whoa! Whoa!" he said. "Slow down. I can't hear

you when you're all yelling. What's wrong? And please don't tell me the cows are loose again."

"No," Hannah said. "They're in their stalls, out of the storm."

Abe was thankful for that bit of news.

"But Fern isn't," Annie said. "She's gone."

He rubbed his temple as Caleb and Levi came around, and he silently prayed it wasn't another broken latch. He'd never seen so many animals escape from their enclosures. Yesterday, it was chickens. The day before, it'd been Hurly the draft horse. This morning, fifteen goats. It was a good thing they gathered near line of trees where dry leaves blanketed the ground or it might have taken hours to gather them. Thankfully, they had gathered around the foliage and snacked, making them easy to capture.

"How'd Fern get loose?" Caleb asked.

"She didn't," Sara said.

"Can you please tell us what's going on without playing the question game?" Abe sighed. "Why isn't she in her stall?"

"Naomi and the buggy are gone, too," Annie said.

He kept his frustrated growl in check. "Now, why couldn't you have said that in the first place?"

Sara shrugged.

"What about Daniel and Zeke?" Abe asked, already knowing the answer.

"Gone," Hannah said.

Thunder shook the barn, and Abe looked out the double barn doors. Lightning lit up the darkening sky. Lighter gray clouds, hanging in wisps, drifted with the wind.

"Bad storm, *jah*?" Levi asked beside him.

"*Jah*, haven't seen one this bad in years." Abe's heart pounded in his chest. Where was she? The thought of her out in this storm scared him, and all he wanted to do was see her, hold her and never let her go.

"Did she leave a note?" Levi asked.

Abe ran out of the barn, knowing Naomi would have left one on the kitchen table.

"No, but she finished cleaning the flower bed," Sara said.

Abe stopped, feeling deflated and slightly guilty at not having been there to help. That should have been something they'd done together as *mann* and *fraa*. It was something he'd wanted to do with her, but he was too much of a coward to spend any more time with her. He raked his hand beneath his hat. Frustration dug into him like a patch of cockleburs. "Where'd she go?"

"If we knew, we'd tell you," Sara said with more sarcasm than normal, which told him she was scared.

He pulled her against his side, trying to be careful not to get her dirty. "We'll find her and the boys."

"The pie is gone," Annie added.

"Pie?" he asked, raising his brow. That at least told him something and gave him hope. "Who would she visit?"

They looked at him blankly with their mouths open. "If she went to visit a neighbor, maybe they're not in the storm but at someone's house."

"She doesn't go visiting," Hannah said. "She hasn't since *Mamm* and *Daed* died."

"Our parents are the closest neighbors she has," Levi said.

Abe's heart stopped. Had she gone to see *Mamm*? Another crack of thunder rocked the barn with such force it shook the ground. An alarming whistle hummed through the roof sheeting. "Levi, take them all to the house. Go to the basement if you need to. I'm going to find Naomi and the boys."

He climbed onto the tractor and turned the key. The motor roared to life, and he backed it out of the barn. Rain sliced against him and pounded the ground, turning it into a swamp. He prayed the tractor didn't get stuck and make a bad situation worse, because if Naomi had gone to see his parents, *Daed* would have made her and the boys leave no matter what the weather. He pulled out onto the road and headed toward his parents' farm, praying he'd find them quickly. The tractor wasn't very fast, even in its highest gear, and would take too long to drive the two miles.

Hail the size of grape tomatoes pummeled the ground. Small bits of branches from the barren tall cottonwoods growing along the road flew over and around him. A branch the size of his arm rolled across the road and tangled in barbed wire. No one in their right mind should be out in this weather. But he was determined to find Naomi and the boys.

He hunkered under the brim of his hat and tried to keep the rain from stinging his eyes. A horse with a white mane and tail flew past him. Fern. But where was the buggy? He didn't have to wait long to find out. A mile from his *daed*'s farm, he saw the black conveyance lying on its side in the middle of the gravel road. "No!"

He jumped off the tractor and trudged through the mud as fast as he could, his boots slipping and sliding while the mud sucked at his soles. He fell against the buggy and looked inside then dropped to his knees, clawing his way inside. It was empty. He scrambled back out and unfolded to his full height. He spun in circles, glancing around for any movement or place where they might have taken shelter.

"Naomi!" he bellowed at the top of his lungs. Nothing. "Naomi!"

A large old oak, rotten at the trunk, gave way beneath the weight of the wind and crashed to the ground. "*Gotte!* Please, help me! Where are they?"

For some reason, 1 Corinthians chapter 13 rushed through his thoughts, coming at him like the 80 mph winds ambushing the land and whipping around him.

Naomi had held no account of wrongs against him; she'd even given him forgiveness when he least deserved it. She faced him head-on with brave courage, and as far as he knew, she'd done the same with those who gossiped behind her back.

Abe's heart thudded in his throat because fear over Naomi and the boys' safety wracked his body. He fell to his knees and clawed at the mud, screaming at the top of his lungs. Fear of his *daed* had held him most of his life, but this fear of losing Naomi and the boys was worse. "*Gotte*, if they are well, if they are safe, I will tell her I love her and the reason I had to leave, I promise, and I will stay if she lets me."

The rain lessened, and he climbed to his feet. He took another look around for any place they might have hidden. "Naomi, Daniel, Zeke!"

The soft pitter-patter of rain kissing the ground was the only sound. The raging storm followed by the soft, gentle drops of rain reminded him of *Mamm* defying their father to bring him and Levi peanut butter and jelly sandwiches while they smelled like skunks. *Mamm*'s kindness had been there, even in the face of the storm.

Fear had driven him away from Garnett. Fear drove him away from Naomi and the love she offered him, and he didn't want fear to control him anymore. If he was going to stay, he'd have to do the same: offer his *mamm* and *daed* forgiveness. Even if they didn't accept it or want it. Just as it had been Naomi's choice to forgive him, it had to be his to forgive his *daed*. That didn't mean he had to subject himself or his family to his father's abuse or anger. It just meant, with *Gotte*'s help, his heart would be free of fear and free to love. That was the only way forward for him, for him and Naomi and the *kinder*. He prayed he would find Naomi and the boys alive and well. He prayed he got the chance to love her, and love her well.

Chapter Eleven

Naomi sat at the small, round kitchen table with Zeke on her lap and Daniel on the floor beside her, fear still quaking through every part of her. She didn't think the adrenaline would ever leave. It would be a constant reminder of how close she and the boys had come to death. If it hadn't been for Abe's *daed*, they just might have. "*Denki* for the blankets and hot coffee."

"Henry shouldn't have let you leave in the storm," Abe's *mamm* said.

"I'm grateful he came to our rescue." Naomi blew the rising steam from her coffee then took a sip to ease the chill seeping through her wet clothes.

"He never should have let you leave," Martha repeated as she examined Naomi. "You're not hurt?"

Shaking her head, Naomi said, "No, only scared."

Fern had come close enough to kicking her that her hoof had ripped Naomi's skirt.

"I put my foot down. Said something for a change. Made him go."

Naomi searched the kitchen and family room for Henry, but he had gone. She noticed how sparse the rooms were of furniture. Only two chairs graced the kitchen table, and there were only wooden rockers in the living room with a side table in between them. Light flickered inside the old hurricane lamp, illuminating a tattered black Bible. Henry threw some logs into the fireplace and lit it before he sulked out the door.

She'd been surprised at the hand grabbing the reins, and even more surprised when she noticed it was Abe's *daed.* He'd stopped their horse from bolting after the lightning struck and then helped her release the buggy from her harness. He had smacked Fern's rump so she understood she could run free. Then he lifted both boys from the buggy and placed them on the tractor only seconds before the wind tossed the buggy down the road. Her earlier encounter with him had both angered her and frightened her, and if she'd had a choice, she would have declined his help out of fear of what he might say or do. But she'd been more scared of the storm and what might happen to her and the boys.

"I ran to the phone hut and called my *schwester.* She owns this farm, you know?"

"Aunt Esther?"

Abe's *mamm* scratched her nail at a mark on the table. "Our *daed* gave it to her, but she didn't want to live here." She gazed at Zeke with such tenderness and longing it nearly tore at Naomi's heart. "He won't hurt my little boys anymore. He won't hurt you, either."

Naomi gasped and tightened her hold on Zeke. Her heart hurt at the thought of anyone hurting *kinder.* She tilted her head and tried to comprehend what she was saying. It was obvious Martha spoke about Abe and Levi, but she wasn't sure who had hurt them. Henry? She'd seen his anger and heard his threats. But had he hurt Abe and Levi? Is that what Martha meant?

"Their *daed* was a *gut* man."

Daniel tapped his hand on the wooden floor, and Zeke wriggled on Naomi's lap. She looked around, just to make sure Henry hadn't entered unnoticed. She let Zeke down but kept her hand on his shoulder to keep him from wandering too far. Abe's *mamm* seemed to be trying to tell her something important, and she didn't want to be distracted by the boys, but it was hard to keep focus with the cold permeating her skin. It was overwhelming, and no matter how tight she pulled the borrowed blanket around herself, she couldn't chase away the shivers. She glanced at the boys, thankful they seemed to be warm enough.

"He was a *gut*, *gut* man." Martha sipped her coffee, got up from the table and cut pieces of pie from the tin on the stovetop. Naomi sipped the bitter coffee, wishing she had some sweetener.

"He would have let me see my *sohn* marry his beautiful *fraa*."

Naomi's hands trembled, and her coffee cup clattered to the table.

"Who?" Naomi's hands trembled, and her coffee cup clattered to the table.

"Abe's *fater*."

Naomi's brow furrowed in confusion since Abe's father had come to the ceremony and Martha hadn't.

A loud knock sounded on the door, and Martha shuffled to open it. She smiled. "I knew you'd come. I cut you a piece of pie," she said.

Naomi was puzzled by the woman's strange behavior after the storm, but her relief overwhelmed her when Abe walked in, wet and muddy. She sagged against the chair and closed her eyes. *Denki, Gotte!*

"Ba, Ba!" Daniel scrambled to his feet, dropped his blanket and ran to Abe.

Abe swung Daniel into his arms and hugged him close, never once taking his eyes off Naomi. "*Gut daag*, little guy."

Naomi's heart swelled at her *bruder*'s excitement to see Abe.

"We scared." Zeke jumped up and went to Abe and wrapped his arms around his leg.

Still holding Daniel, Abe kneeled and said, "I was scared, too." He hugged him tightly. "I'm glad you are okay, *jah*?"

Naomi slid from her chair and folded the blanket tighter in front of her. She lifted her chin a little and prepared for his reprimand, but Abe's gaze was soft and warm. He stood, still holding her verbally challenged five-year-old *bruder*, while her active, verbal three-year-old *bruder* clung to his leg. Seeing him standing there, holding her *brudres* with so much care and love, she knew, without any doubt, she loved him.

She looked at Abe's *mamm*, so small and frail and short of mind, and she thought she understood why Abe left, and why he had to leave again. He couldn't remain in the same town with a man like his *daed*. Henry seemed to be a hard man, and she feared he'd caused pain to Abe. She wanted to run to him and hold him and let him know everything would be okay. Abe being here, in the home where he possibly suffered under the hands of his *daed*, made her love him all the more. He'd come here for her, for the boys.

"I am glad to see you are well," he said, breaking the silence over the crackling fire in the family room.

She nodded. "Me, too."

Abe put Daniel down, freed himself from Zeke's hold and closed the distance between them. He wrapped his free arm around her shoulders and pulled her close. She sagged against his strength and trembled. "I'm sorry."

"Don't," he said, his breath warm against her ear. "The storm came on quick. You couldn't have known."

"Come sit," Martha said. "Your *fraa* brought pie."

"Thank you, *Mamm*, but we should get home to the other *kinder*." Releasing her, Abe gazed into her eyes. "Are you *oll recht*?"

Naomi nodded. "*Jah*, still scared but *oll recht*."

"I don't think I'll ever shake my fear after seeing the buggy rolled on its side in the middle of the road." He drew his finger down the side of her jaw. "Thank *Gotte* you're not hurt."

"Your *daed* rescued us," she said.

Abe's brow shot up.

"That man is not my boys' *fater*," Martha said.

Abe and Naomi snapped their gazes to her.

"He's my husband, not their *daed*."

Naomi grabbed hold of Abe's hand and willed him to look at her. She would be his strength and his rock as he'd been hers the last few weeks.

"I'm here, Abe. Right by your side."

Abe listened to *Mamm* as she told them about his real *fater* and how he'd died in a farming accident when Abe was four and Levi in his mother's womb and how she married Henry Dienner, his real *fater*'s second cousin, shortly after the accident to help support herself and her *kinder*.

"Henry wasn't always a hard man. He laughed and

played with you boys. We looked forward to more *bopplis*, but none came. He wanted boys of his own."

"That isn't cause to hurt little ones," Naomi pointed out.

His *mamm* stared into her empty cup. "No, but I didn't know how to stop it. I didn't know I could ask for help. From childhood, I was taught to submit to my husband."

Abe reached across the table and covered his *mamm*'s hand. "It's *oll recht, Mamm*."

She shook her head. "I should have talked to the bishop, but I was scared."

"As you had every right to be," Naomi said.

Mamm finally looked up from her coffee cup. "When Jeremiah showed up and saw Levi's broken arm, he brought the bishop back, and they confronted Henry and took Levi with them. I never saw either one of my *sohns* again until Abe showed up last week. Their absence made me realize how much I'd missed them and how wrong I'd been not to seek help. The injury you caused to Henry to protect your *bruder* wasn't in anger, Abe. It was in love. You protected Levi." She paused. "I'm sorry for not doing the same for you."

"I forgive you, *Mamm*."

He gave his mother a hug, full of all the love and forgiveness he could muster. It felt freeing to do so.

Shortly after, he helped Naomi and the boys onto the tractor. They rode home in silence. The thrum of the tractor beat in tandem with his thoughts. He wasn't Henry Dienner's son after all! He didn't carry his DNA in his veins. He was free! He glanced behind him and saw the woman he loved and wondered how she felt about the revelation. Would she be able to love him? Would she let him stay?

* * *

Naomi climbed the stairs to the farmhouse with Daniel and Zeke and was met by all her siblings as they gathered around them. They hugged and laughed and cried, and she assured them she and the boys were fine. Hannah had a warm bath ready and took the boys so Naomi could change her clothes and warm by the stove.

Soon, she stood at the kitchen window, towel drying her hair, watching for any sign of Abe. He, Levi and Caleb had already retrieved the buggy, and she hadn't seen him since. What was Abe feeling right now, after discovering he wasn't his *fater*'s true *sohn*.

Was he angry? Sad? She assumed he was in the barn, and she wanted to go to him, but figured he needed space to sort things out and tell Levi all they'd learned.

Before they'd left Abe's childhood home, Abe's *mamm* assured them she would be fine and the bishop would see to it Henry was removed from the house until he received the proper counseling through the church. She didn't know if Henry Dienner would ever return, but at least Abe could rest well knowing his *mamm* would be safe for a while.

Naomi stopped drying her hair as she saw Abe exit the barn, his tattered suitcase in his hand.

She felt the sting of tears against her eyes. Was this it? Was he leaving?

She stepped out onto the porch. Blue skies had replaced the storm clouds, and if it weren't for the broken tree limbs scattered about, no one would believe a storm had just blown through town.

"Gut daag," she said as he propped a boot onto the bottom step.

"*Gut daag*, Naomi."

She eyed his suitcase with trepidation, scared to ask him if he was leaving. She knew he had to go. She understood Garnett held too much pain for him. But she didn't want him to leave. She loved him with every fiber of her being, but because she loved him, she had to let him.

Abe set his suitcase on the top step and reached his hand out to her. "Will you join me a moment?"

She draped the towel over the rail and took his hand. They walked through the muddy yard until they came to the bench *Daed* had made for *Mamm* to sit on. Someone had dried it, and he sat, drawing her down beside him.

"You've learned a lot about me today," he said.

"I already knew what was important, Abe."

"And what was that?"

She touched her palm to his bearded jaw, drawing him to look at her. His eyes held doubt and hesitation. "You're the kindest and most thoughtful man. You're full of love and compassion." She paused a moment, feeling her own doubt creep in, but she gathered her courage and forged ahead. "And *ich lieba dich.*"

"Even after all you know about me, my family?"

"None of that has changed what I already knew. You are a *gut* man, Abe Dienner, and a *wunderbar* husband."

They sat in silence for a few minutes. He lifted his hand and pointed toward a large lone cloud. "It looks like a heart." He glanced at her. "My heart for you and the *kinder.*"

Her breath hitched in her throat. Did he love her?

He dropped to one knee in front of her and took her hands in his. "*Ich lieba dich*, Naomi. I have for a long time. Would you be my *fraa* for real? May I move into the house, and work with you on the farm each day, and rest my head on the pillow beside you each night for the rest of our lives?"

She smiled and said, "Only if you promise to kiss me *gut* morning every day."

"That's a promise I can keep," he said as he folded her into his arms and kissed her.

Cheers and claps erupted around them, and they broke apart. They were surrounded by the *kinder* and Levi.

"Does this mean we can be a real family?" Sara asked.

"*Jah*, it does," Abe answered before kissing Naomi one more time.

"It means he'll be staying," Hannah said.

"Woo-hoo!" Caleb hollered.

"Does that mean we can quit letting the animals out and breaking the clothesline?" Annie asked.

"Annie!" the *kinder* said in tandem.

Abe pulled back and looked at Naomi with a shocked, questioning expression.

She shrugged. "I guess they really wanted you to stay."

"Nothing could make me leave," he said before kissing her one more time.

Epilogue

Naomi hung the last of Abe's shirts onto the clothesline and stood back to admire the array of colors. It was hard to imagine it'd only been seven months ago the line displayed a lot of black and white. And although their official time of mourning had ended in January, she still missed her parents.

"Liebling," Abe said as he came up behind her and wrapped his arms around her midsection. The *boppli* in her womb tumbled around. "What are you doing?"

She smiled and rested her hands on his. It did not matter what troubles there were; as long as Abe was near, she knew all would be well. "Admiring the clothesline."

"You like it, *jah*?"

"Jah, it is *wunderbar*." The old posts had been a victim to a strong storm last week. Abe, Caleb and Levi dug new holes and placed new posts in the ground. "I like the pulley system, so I don't have to walk around on the unsteady ground. *Denki*."

"We wouldn't want you to fall in your state."

Naomi laughed. "My state is quite normal, *liebling*. And what are you doing, *mann*? Shouldn't you be in the fields?"

"*Ach, jah*, you're quite a taskmaster, but we have a surprise for you."

"We?" She looked up at him in surprise.

"Your *brudres* and *schwesters*, Levi and my *mamm*."

"Oh, what is it?"

"Come," he said as he took her hand and led her to the front yard.

As they turned the corner, she gasped at the colorful display. "Oh, Abe, they're beautiful."

When it was time to plant the flower seeds, she let the *kinder* put them where they wanted. It had taken all her self-control to keep from organizing them and making suggestions, which meant many of the seeds had been scattered from the porch to the barn. Very few had made it to the flower bed, and she had been okay with that. It seemed her self-control and practice in patience had paid off.

The flower bed had several rows of wave petunias, which would spread out and fill the empty spaces.

"Look, Nomi," Zeke said, tugging on her hand and pointed to a corner where violet flowers brightened the dirt.

"I see. It's lovely, Zeke. *Denki*."

"He wanted to plant it in Rose's stall, but I wouldn't let him," Annie said. "Mine are over there. I did the roots just like you showed me." She pointed to a cluster of pink blooms.

"You did *gut*, Annie." She glanced around at her family and knew this was *Gotte*'s will, even though they'd gone through much sadness and difficulties to get here. As mismatched as they were, they were family. Abe's *mamm* had blossomed over the last several months and she'd been a big help around the house on the days she came to visit. Her *schwesters* looked forward to baking days with Martha.

"Martha, Rachel and I did the rest," Sarah said. "We thought you'd like the bright red ones in the center."

"It's beautiful. *Denki*, everyone."

"We're not done," Abe said.

"Nae?" Naomi asked.

"Go," Daniel said as he tugged on her hand. She beamed down at him. When Abe came back into their lives, Naomi wasn't sure why Daniel all of a sudden tried speaking, but now he was doing *wunderbar*, even if he only spoke a few words.

"Jah," Caleb said as he ran toward the row of redbud trees. They'd long lost their beautiful purple blooms, but the heart-shaped leaves remained vibrant and green.

"Race you," Annie hollered. Little Daniel released her hand and chased after his *brudres* and *schwesters*, even Rachel and Sara took off, their bare feet kicking up into the air. Levi snagged Zeke off his feet, and Abe's *mamm* inched up her dress and ran after them, too.

Naomi put her hand in Abe's as they strolled through the yard. "It's *gut* to see your *mamm* happy, *jah*?"

"For sure and for certain," Abe said. "My *fraa* has given her a lot to be happy about, *jah*?"

Naomi wouldn't contradict him, but she knew it had a lot to do with him, too, and the love he offered to his *mamm*. "She is family."

"Jah," Abe said, his eyes focusing on the large group ahead of them. "What a *wunderbar* family, too. Now close your eyes, my *liebling*."

She did, trusting him to help her navigate the steps

with her uneven footing. Just as she would trust him to help navigate their future.

He turned her and she immediately sensed the shade of the redbuds, shielding the bench *Daed* had made for *Mamm*.

"You can open your eyes now," he whispered near her ear.

She did and gaped. "*Ach du lieva*, it's—it's *wunderbar*."

Two wooden flower boxes were positioned on either side of the bench. Bright, colorful flowers and various shades of green vines spilled over, several more were placed to form an arc on either side. A large quilt laid out in the center with a basket on the corner.

She didn't know what to say.

"Hannah, Levi and I made the containers," Caleb said, smiling.

"And we," Annie said, motioning to Rachel and Abe's *mamm*, "planted the flowers."

"It was *gut* to be part of this surprise," Martha said.

"*Denki,*" Naomi said. "It's *gut* to have you be a part of our lives."

"We know how much this area means to you," Abe said.

She choked back the sob forming in her throat, but she couldn't stop the tears from spilling over the edge of her lashes. "It was *Mamm*'s favorite place to read and to pray."

Sara moved forward; her fingers knotted together. "You've done so much for us, Naomi. Keeping us together in our home. We wanted you to have a special place, and we did this together as a family."

Hot tears trailed down Naomi's cheeks, and she pulled

Sara into a hug. Sara had to do a lot of growing up for an eleven year old, and it seemed once she was assured they would continue to be a family and Abe wouldn't leave, her tantrums had lessened. "*Ich lieba dich*, Sara."

"Don't forget about the last surprise, Sara," Abe said.

"*Ach*," Sara said, pulling away. She and Abe disappeared behind a white sheet hanging between two redbuds, and when they reappeared, they brought with them a beautifully made bassinet. "We know the *boppli* won't be here for a few months, but we couldn't wait to give it to you."

"We all helped, but Sara did a lot. She was good at finding the right pieces of wood, and I found this in your *daed*'s shop."

Abe pulled a box from inside the bassinet. The corner joints were perfect dovetails, just like *Daed* made them.

"There is a note inside." He handed it to Naomi.

She slid the off the lid, and saw her *daed*'s distinct scrawl. *Naomi and Abe, may your union be as blessed with unending and unconditional* lieb, *much forgiveness and grace, and with as many* wunderbar kinder *as your* mamm *and I have. With much* lieb, Mamm *and* Daed.

"*Ach*," she said, no longer able to hold back the sobs. If she couldn't have her parents around to celebrate her marriage with Abe and to welcome her first *boppli*, this was the next best thing. "*Denki*, everyone for blessing me, and *denki* for making *Mamm* and *Daed* a part of this special day." They may not have been there for the ceremony, just as Martha hadn't been, but this was special, surrounded by the people she loved most. It was a day she would not soon forget.

She stretched up on her toes and kissed Abe's cheek. "*Denki*, my *wunderbar mann. Ich lieba dich.*"

"*Ich lieba dich*, my *fraa.*"

* * * * *

Dear Reader,

I hope you enjoyed Abe and Naomi's story and this introduction to Garnett, Kansas. When I first thought about writing an Amish story, I knew I wanted to place the story in Kansas. The Garnett Amish community was established in the early 1900s. And yes, they do drive tractors. This book wouldn't have been possible without the help of friends from the area and AmishAmerica.com who documented this particular community online. Any mistakes are purely my own.

I realize that my book touches on the sensitive subject of abuse, but abuse happens, and more often than we know. Abuse is no respecter of persons. It knows no gender or age. It does not recognize religions or faiths. It can happen within any family or within any church organization. I wanted to show how abuse affected my hero, and how manipulation and fear can control a person's actions. Abe fears for the well-being of his family, but more importantly he fears becoming just like his father. He is always worried about others, which is why he keeps the secret of abuse and doesn't ask for help.

If you find yourself in a similar situation, please reach out for help. Call the National Domestic Violence Hotline at 1-800-799-7233 or text 88788.

I love hearing from readers. You can contact me through my website at www.authorchristinarich.com. You can also find me on Facebook at AuthorChristinaRich or on Instagram at author_christina_rich.

Thanks!
Christina Rich

HARLEQUIN
Reader Service

Enjoyed your book?

Try the perfect subscription for Romance readers and get more great books like this delivered right to your door.

See why over 10+ million readers have tried Harlequin Reader Service.

Start with a Free Welcome Collection with free books and a gift—valued over $20.

Choose any series in print or ebook.
See website for details and order today:

TryReaderService.com/subscriptions